UNREMEDIED

Carol J. Roth

Everything I do is made possible by my loving family. Anitra, Neil, Astrid, Vee—thank you.

PROLOGUE: MAISIE

The pond was a pool of blood. The setting sun bathed its surface in a pure red glow.

The woman writhed in her captor's arms, and the suddenness of her movement made up for her small frame and heavy, protruding belly. He tried to clamp down on her but couldn't adjust his grip in time, and she broke free.

She didn't go far; just to the oak tree at the edge of the water. He caught up to her as she wrapped her arms around another man, tall and lanky, his clothes a little loose on him. Her dress was ill-fitting too, tight across her chest, the waist hiked up to the area between her breasts and belly. Because of this adjustment, it was shorter in front, and her incongruously slender calves and ankles showed, as did her worn and dusty shoes. Her dark hair tumbled loose around her face, any semblance of order long gone.

The three struggled wordlessly, making only grunts and inarticulate sounds, while others around them stood momentarily frozen. The lanky man pressed against the pregnant woman as best he could, but his hands were tied behind his back, and whenever he strayed too far from where he stood, the rope around his neck tightened warningly. The woman's frantic embrace nearly knocked him into one of the two other men in nooses who stood on either side of him, but he didn't push her away, even when he wheezed and had to straighten hastily to relieve the pressure on his throat.

The first man succeeded in pulling the woman away, and she found her voice at last. "George!" That was all she managed before she broke into hoarse, ugly sobs.

"Don't worry, Maisie," the lanky man said, in a feeble attempt at bravery. He took a shuddering breath. "We can settle this, fellers. It ain't got to be like this."

Another man spoke up. "Ain't nothing a goddamn horse thief can say to get his neck outta the noose."

"You know I ain't stole nothing, Peterson," George said, his hands straining against their bonds. "None of us did. We traded for them horses back at the fort." His breath shook in a way that sounded almost like a laugh. "You're the horse thief. Just admit it, take everything, and leave me and my family alone."

Peterson scratched his stubble. "I *could* take back what's rightfully mine and let you go," he mused. "Problem with that is, we let you live, you're gonna keep causing me trouble by spreading lies. And word might get around that we're soft on horse thieves in these parts. No," he said, with finality, "they's only one way to handle this."

A burst of movement to his left caused him to draw his gun. One of the other prisoners had managed to get his hands free and pull the noose off his own neck. Peterson lunged and brought the butt of his pistol down on the young man's head before he could run, and he fell. Maisie shrieked. Peterson's other man kicked him repeatedly in the stomach and chest as Peterson pistol-whipped him. His cries grew increasingly wheezing and faint as he struggled to draw breath in.

"My son!" George roared, struggling harder against his restraints. "Let him be! Don't hurt him!"

"Charlie, Charlie," Maisie moaned. The man on the other side of George—a boy, really—seemed on the verge of hanging himself; his knees buckled and he swayed, his face ghostly pale, as if he might faint.

Peterson stepped back, panting a little. He straightened his hat, which had been knocked askew. "Get him back up there, Marsters," he said in a flat voice to the man who'd joined him in his attack.

Marsters hauled Charlie to his feet. The young man's eyes were glazed and his hair was darkly matted with blood where the pistol had struck him. He sagged in Marsters's arms, his head sometimes drooping as if he were nodding off before he blinked and straightened with a puzzled expression. His eyes rested briefly on each person's face, showing no more recognition of his family than of the other men. George groaned when his son's gaze passed blankly over him.

Marsters dragged Charlie back to where the empty noose dangled. With one arm holding the young man upright, he worked the rope back over his head and positioned it under his chin. He looked expectantly at Peterson, keeping hold of Charlie so he didn't collapse.

Peterson nodded, and Marsters pulled on the loose end of the rope, grunting with effort. Charlie's feet slowly left the ground. Unspeakable sounds accompanied the moans of his family as he choked and twitched.

Before his death throes were over, Peterson strode over to the even younger man amid George's protestations to leave him be. The boy tried to skitter away but his noose made it impossible. As Peterson put his full weight on the rope and the noose tightened, the boy danced on tiptoes for a few seconds before he too lost contact with the earth. His struggles were more strenuous than Charlie's had been, which hastened the process of asphyxiation.

"Don't—don't," Maisie panted. "Johnny. Oh Johnny." She leaned forward and retched, producing nothing more than strings of bitter bile that clung to her lower lip before dripping to the ground. The man holding her recoiled and, feeling his grip loosen, she pulled away again, this time running straight at Peterson. She knocked him back a few steps and the noose dropped, as did the boy hanging from it. Johnny collapsed on the ground wheezing faintly, his arms and legs jerking slightly.

Peterson punched Maisie hard in her protruding stomach and she clutched it protectively with terror in her eyes. He used her momentary helplessness to draw his pistol and shoot her. The bullet tore through her left arm and into her side, about where her belly started to slope outward.

Maisie looked down at her arm, which now hung uselessly, then up at the man who'd shot her. It was her turn to crumple to the ground, red stains ballooning on the sleeve and skirt of her dress. Her one good hand held her belly until her eyes dulled and closed and her right arm fell to the side.

Mercifully, she didn't witness the final dying moments of her husband's two barely grown sons, or George's desolate grief and fury before he, too, was hauled off his feet and slowly strangled. Peterson and his men dragged the bodies of George and his boys to the pond and heaved them into the foul water. They left the nooses around their necks so if anyone found them, they'd assume them to be rustlers or worse.

They avoided looking at the woman until after they'd disposed of the men. "Whaddaya think, boss?" Marsters finally asked, jerking his head at where she lay, near the base of the tree where her family had been hanged.

Peterson reluctantly crouched next to her and leaned down to see if she was breathing.

He looked up with a grimace. "She ain't gonna make it," he said with a hint of guilt in his voice. "Just as well—who's gonna want a widow with a bastard?" He shook his head. "She shouldn't'a run at me like that." His tone hardened. "Leave her be—she'll be dead before we're a mile away. You all saw that tall feller reach for my gun and shoot her with it by accident, right?"

The other two muttered assent, uneasy and ready to leave the scene. After rifling through the battered wagon's meager contents for anything worth taking, they unhooked the horses, tied leads on them, and mounted their own, trotting back to the trading post in the gathering darkness.

* * *

Agony—a pain so sharp it could bring a woman from the brink of death, at least momentarily. Maisie's eyes blinked open just in time to squeeze shut again as another contraction ripped through her abdomen. Her throat was dry and her cry was husky and cracked.

She half crawled, half dragged herself to the pond's edge and drank deeply of the brackish water, grimacing at its taste and smell but unable to resist the urge to slake her thirst.

As she lifted her head, her eyes met another's. She scrabbled backward, not immediately recognizing George's face as it bobbed out of the water in the moonlight, wide-eyed, distorted and disfigured by his slow strangulation.

Maisie couldn't scream at first, but a contraction forced one out of her, weak and breathy. Every muscle felt frail from the pain and blood loss, except the ones deep within her that instinctively fought to bring forth her child. Those muscles strained again and again, and with each push, more blood seeped out of her wounds, slower and thicker now.

The pain between her legs surpassed that of her arm and side. Her screams at every contraction were nearly silent now. There were hardly any breaks now before the irresistible pressure built up again and she pushed, her baby and her life inching out of her a little more each time.

* * *

She managed to prop herself up against the tree trunk afterward. Her baby suckled and slept, oblivious to the horror around it.

Maisie was calm too. She looked around and saw in the leaves a piece of paper. She couldn't read the untidily printed words but she knew what it was—Peterson's farce of a wanted notice.

With the baby nestled against her shattered left arm, she felt around with her right, found a slender twig, and snapped it against the ground to create a sharp point. The blood on her clothes and still seeping from her wound was viscous and drying rapidly, so she worked fast, dipping the twig in it and scratching out words on the back of the notice. She ran out of space, ink, and energy at about the same time, gave the paper a messy one-handed fold, and tucked it into the shawl she'd wrapped her infant in, placenta and all. With the last of her strength—her vision and consciousness seemed to be receding, backing away into a dark and endless tunnel—she lifted a leather cord from around her neck, at the end of which dangled a curious silver shape, and pushed that too into the folds of material enclosing her baby.

Maisie tried to pray. She tried to remember the good times with George and her stepsons. She tried to savor the feel of her baby in her arms. But her mind was dull and scattered, and the end of her earthly consciousness was a vague, confused memory of a toothache she'd once had.

* * *

The baby's tiny pealing cries weren't audible over the rattling of the passing wagon, but George's abandoned vehicle caught the attention of the people walking along next to it. As they sorted dutifully through the already picked-over contents—it wasn't the first one they'd passed, and it was always worth a look—the renewed cries, interrupted only by fruitless suckling of the cold breast it was nestled against, caused one of the men to look around. His horrified shout once he found the source of the sound brought his compatriots running.

They looked with dismay and pity at the macabre tableau, a nightmarish mimicry of Madonna and child. At last one of them pried the swaddled and squalling child out of Maisie's stiff arms, opened the blanket to inspect it, and cut the cord that anchored the infant to the placenta, grimacing at the skin mottled with dried blood and a whitish crust.

They could ill afford a break, but they took an hour or so to dig a shallow grave under the oak tree and bury the woman. Then they wrapped the baby back up and carried it as they led their ox-driven wagon along the trail. They'd been so mesmerized by the sight of Maisie and the baby that they didn't spare a glance at the murky pond, or notice the face just below its surface.

* * *

As they walked—preferring that to riding in their wagon, which would bounce them mercilessly against the hard seat as it jolted along the ruts of the trail—one of the men attempted to feed the baby. He'd coaxed about half a cup of milk from their scrawny goat and dipped the cleanest piece of cloth he could find in his belongings in it, then tried to get the baby suck on the fabric. It was a frustrating method for both of them, but eventually the child seemed to grasp what was being offered, gumming the cloth hungrily for every possible drop. The man dipped it in the milk again and again, trying not to slosh or tip the cup as he walked and held the baby.

After a while, the men fashioned a sling and took turns wearing it. By the time they reached the next waypoint, a small trading post, lethargy had set in for the small creature. He cried occasionally, but weakly; most of the time the infant slept or stared at nothing with big liquid brown eyes.

At the post they warmed some water in a bucket and gave the boy a bath. The shawl was blood-crusted beyond repair, so they discarded it and wrapped the baby in a threadbare undershirt.

The men regarded the note with puzzlement; neither of them could read, so both sides were indecipherable. They stowed it with Maisie's necklace among their things, loath to discard the child's last links to the past.

The wife of the trading post proprietor, in her forties and having had several children who were grown, fashioned a better feeding system with a narrow-mouthed bottle and a cloth tied over the top, and the infant recovered somewhat. "Mother's milk would be better," the woman said, but the men were relieved at the improvement in his condition.

She made a crib out of a small wooden crate, which she kept in her and her husband's bedroom that night, and in the morning she offered to take the child on in hopes that a nursing woman would pass through and agree to take another charge. The men, who had camped in their wagon overnight, acquiesced with relief. They should've been in Wyoming by now. Raising a child had not been part of their plans, and they needed to make up for lost time if they were to reach California before snow made the journey too difficult. They each stroked the baby's head and let him grip their finger, thanked the woman, and got back onto the trail.

One of them had wrapped the piece of paper and necklace in a kerchief and left it with the trader's wife. She examined the piece of jewelry. Two oblong oval loops were interwoven to form a kind of cross, except all four ends were of equal length.

The woman could read, so she perused the side of the paper detailing the horse thievery charges. That could explain how the mother had gotten herself killed, if she were mixed up with thieves. The other side of the paper, written in its ghastly makeshift ink, was a mystery. Either it was in another language or the woman who had scrawled it had been too delirious to write anything intelligible.

The baby stayed with her for two weeks, living on cow's milk, not thriving but not declining either. Finally a wagon party came through with a new mother who had only managed to produce her first child after many miscarriages and a difficult pregnancy. Afraid she might not be able to have many (or any) more children of her own, she and her husband agreed to make the boy part of their family.

The trader's wife told a much milder form of the baby's story to the new adoptive mother; she didn't want to saddle the younger woman with such haunting images as she tried to bond with the wee thing herself.

She passed along the two talismans given to her by the men who had discovered the baby. She had no idea if the new mother would want to erase the infant's past and raise him as her own. The trader's wife was curious, but she didn't ask. The young woman was probably having enough conflicted and complicated feelings as it was without having to decide that, or defend her decision if she already knew what she was going to do. The older woman was just grateful the child would be getting human milk again.

She felt a tug of sadness. The pale little creature had grown on her. At the same time, she had enough to do helping her husband with his business, and generating additional income by selling cooked meals and hand-sewn clothes and supplies. She didn't need to start the parenting process all over again. She also felt she'd never be able to shake the tale the men had told of their grim discovery of the baby. Sometimes, despite reminding herself that the worst of the horror had all taken place before the birth had even taken place, she even fancied she saw a haunted, knowing look in the boy's otherwise innocent and oblivious eyes.

1: BARRETT

When the sun reached its highest point in the sky, Barrett found shelter under a tree.

He spread his duster on the ground and laid out his lunch, cured beef and a plain baked potato he'd cooked the night before. He alternated bites so the salty meat and bland potato balanced out on his taste buds. As he munched patiently, he pulled an ancient deck of cards from a pocket of the duster and dealt poker hands against an imaginary opponent. His canteen was running low, but he'd be able to refill it from the well at his next stop, so he allowed himself to drink it nearly down to empty.

Barrett had spent the morning visiting farms on his way out of town and, after he made sure old Ike Weathers was doing all right, he'd take a different route home so he could make another set of stops. He tried to visit the homesteads around town regularly, though not usually this many in one day.

He untied a small packet of dried apple slices once his meat and potato were eaten. Dropping one into his mouth, he scanned the horizon absentmindedly. His thoughts were on earlier that morning.

He'd treated himself to breakfast at the Silver Dollar Saloon, secretly hoping for a chance encounter with Anneleigh—Annie, he called her sometimes, a little shyly, when they were alone. There was no sign of her, but his failed plan did put him in the right place at the right time to meet a wild-eyed stranger.

The man, who eventually introduced himself as Wally, had burst through the door of the Silver Dollar, which was the first establishment travelers would encounter as they entered the town of Harlan from the west. He went straight to the bar. "Whiskey," he said breathlessly, and Billy set him up, unfazed. The burly owner-operator was used to men whose own supply had run dry in their travels and who were starving for a stiff drink.

The man tossed it back, slapped some coins on the bar and turned around. "Where can I find the law around here?" he said loudly to the entire room. No one even had to answer; all eyes turned to Barrett, and the stranger followed the stares. The sheriff sighed and polished off his last bite of steak and eggs as the man hurried toward his table. "What can I do for you, son?"

"Sheriff," he said, pausing dramatically. "You've got a madman running loose in these here parts!"

Remembering, Barrett chuckled a little to himself, shaking his head, and ate another apple slice. It wasn't a wasted day to check in on his constituency, but he might feel a little foolish by the time he got home that night, caked in dust and sweat. He wondered if Anneleigh would still be available by the time he got washed up and dressed in his good shirt and trousers, or if she'd already have a different customer by then.

He was still skeptical of Wally's claim of a deranged lunatic attacking him—*biting* him, he said, and he did have a ragged wound in his right forearm, though it was hard to believe a man had done it. And everyone Barrett had visited thus far had been fine, hadn't seen anything unusual.

So why am I still out here? The question materialized, but he had no clear answer for himself. People came to him with complaints and charges of all kinds, and over the years he'd gotten more and more confident about instinctively weeding out the ones that didn't ring true to him. It didn't have anything to do with how outlandish they were, either; things happened out here in Nevada that he couldn't have imagined growing up on his pa's farm in Tennessee.

It wasn't that he believed Wally to be telling the truth exactly. That wasn't what convinced him to spend a whole day riding in the hot sun, enduring the confused stares of everyone he asked about the alleged attacker.

No, it wasn't Wally's story, which made no sense. And it wasn't his wound—which did look pretty serious, though the man seemed more concerned with justice being served than finding a doctor. It was Barrett's gut. That's what had brought him out on this errand when he'd rather be loitering near the social club, hoping to spot Anneleigh and secure her company for the night.

His dried apple slices were gone. Barrett sighed and lay back, staring at the leaves of the tree above him, lingering a little longer. Partly he was giving his left hip more time to rest—it had never been the same since *another* drifter, drunk and erratic, had shot him one night as Barrett tried to help Billy eject him from the Silver Dollar.

But another part of him wanted to stay so he could drift off dreaming of Anneleigh, of that special orange-scented water she spritzed herself with, which her whole room in the social club seemed to be suffused with. He smiled a little under his thick mustache. Maybe he could find out where to order that stuff from and surprise her with a bottle of it this Christmas. Would it be too familiar, too presumptuous of him? Maybe by Christmas they'd be close enough to make it appropriate, though he'd have to send for it long before then …

He roused himself from that particular train of thought, which was as nerve-wracking as it was exciting, and got his things together. Ike tended to nap in the late afternoon, so he oughtn't delay any longer.

* * *

Roscoe's hectic barking should've sent him running straight to the house, Barrett thought later, but he was thirsty and focused on that well. He drew up a pail and drank deeply from the dipper before filling his canteen. Once he'd done that, though, it dawned on him that Ike's dog had been barking the entire time, no break.

He hadn't known him to do that before. There was something about his tone, too. Higher-pitched, not the low growling like when he sensed a stranger coming, nor the excited full-throated barks of greeting when someone he knew drew near.

Barrett decided to take it slow. He left his horse by the well and walked up the slight slope toward the house, fingers caressing his six-shooter in its holster.

The front door hanging askew on one of its leather hinges, *that* made him want to start running. But he forced himself to keep going at the same steady pace.

There was no sound except Roscoe's barking, and no movement, until Barrett put his foot on the first wooden plank of the makeshift steps to the porch. It creaked minutely and the dog came barreling out of the house. Ordinarily he would've bounded straight to Barrett and leapt onto him, but he stopped right outside the door, seeming about to plunge toward the sheriff but pulled back by an invisible leash toward the front door. Over and over he repeated this minute dance. He wasn't a young dog, but his frenetic energy made him seem so at the moment.

Dread had been building in the pit of Barrett's stomach, and by now it was like a rock. But at least he felt fairly certain no intruder was in the house, or Roscoe would've been more focused on that, instead of seeming to be coaxing the sheriff to come in, come see, now now now.

Barrett climbed the few rickety stairs and pushed the broken front door fully open so he could step into the room he knew well, a combination kitchen and sitting room. The only other rooms in the shack were a bedroom, which Ike used to share with his wife Maggie, and a storage room that was half pantry, half everything they couldn't fit in their other two rooms.

Before he even registered what his eyes saw, he was struck by the squelch of his boot in something thick and viscous on the pine plank floor. He glanced down, saw a no-longer-spreading pool of blood, and moved his gaze along to its origin, a splayed and mangled caricature of a sweetly cantankerous old man that nearly everyone in town was simultaneously annoyed and amused by.

Barrett had seen some things, all right. Not like this. His eyes took in small flashes of the scene rather than the whole thing. The face savaged beyond recognition. The entrails or muscles or—he didn't know what to call the reddish ropy mess coming from the torn-open chest and stomach. Roscoe skittering around in the drying blood, still barking frantically but now with a forlorn timbre, because the rescuer he'd brought wasn't rousing his master and putting him back together.

Barrett wanted to run. He wanted to vomit. Instead he checked the other two rooms to make sure they were empty of intruders. Then he came back to the main area and forced himself to look more closely at the remains of a man he'd long considered a neighbor if not quite a friend.

He couldn't say it *wasn't* an animal that'd done this, although he'd never seen anything like it, so focused on the brains, heart and other organs, the extremities nearly untouched. He forced his reeling mind to quiet down and focus, looking for signs among the chaos that might give him clues to what happened.

The prints. He looked at the confusion of footprints and pawprints left in the blood coating the floor. Most of them were his and Roscoe's. He looked for another type of animal print and saw none. Could Ike's faithful dog have done this? He found it impossible to believe—plus there was barely any blood on the mutt's muzzle, and the small traces could have come from sniffing his master's body. The sheriff looked for other human prints besides his own … and there he saw it. Boot prints a little smaller than his, smudged and tracked over but still discernible.

No animal besides Roscoe had been in the room since the blood was spilled, as far as Barrett could tell. But another human had.

* * *

Roscoe wasn't a bloodhound. Who knows what mix of breeds he was—the lawman had never been sure, nor curious enough to think much about it one way or another. But when Barrett started following the bloody boot prints, which he hadn't noticed before with all the barking and the broken front door, Roscoe took right to the trail. When the sheriff went to get his mount from by the well, Roscoe stayed uneasily by the footprints, whining and looking between Barrett and some point in the distance where the prints might lead. As the sheriff neared the house again, on horseback this time, the dog resumed his dance between Barrett and where he wanted the man to go until Barrett reached the foot of the porch stairs, the beginning of the trail.

Visible tracks faded almost immediately, but Roscoe didn't hesitate, nose to the ground just as intently as it had been when Barrett could see the bloody prints. The dog led the man and horse out into the scrubby terrain beyond Ike's farm.

As they continued along together, Barrett thought about what Wally had said about the attacker. A little fellow, shorter than him, not too muscular but possessed of a kind of frenzied energy that made up for his lack of brute strength. It was hard to imagine someone smaller than Wally being capable of the level of violence that had been visited upon poor old Ike, but then it was hard to imagine *anyone* doing that.

The shadows were growing a little long, but the sun still had a long way to go before it set. Roscoe faltered and Barrett thought he'd lost the trail. But the mutt was staring intently ahead. His scruffy fur stuck up all along his back and he emitted a low, long, uneasy whine. Barrett slowed, then dismounted by Roscoe. He saw a figure bent over, kneeling beside something perhaps? Yes, another person, prone on the ground.

As Barrett crept closer undetected, the dog now silent and keeping behind him as it followed, he saw that the body on the ground was struggling, but the one above it was holding it in such a way that it couldn't get up or fight back.

"Hold on there," Barrett called. He wasn't sure what the person—as he got closer he realized it was a very young man—was trying to do, but he had to put a stop to it.

The young man looked up and saw him. Barrett wasn't yet close enough to make out his expression—the sheriff's long-distance sight wasn't what it once was—but the figure didn't seem to register any alarm or much interest in his approach. Instead the boy looked back down at the helplessly writhing figure under his control, pulled a knife out of a sheath on his belt, and drove it into the top of the other person's skull.

"Hey!" Barrett ran toward the two. "Hands off him, now! Drop it! Git your hands up!" He came to a stop a few feet away, drawing his gun and aiming it at the assailant.

By then he was close enough to see the boy's face clearly. The lad looked as if he were gradually coming out of a trance. He placed the bloody knife on the ground and raised his hands, straightening slowly to a standing position.

"I don't want no trouble," the strange young man said. He had large, dark liquid eyes, smooth tanned skin, and a soft voice in a higher register than the sheriff was expecting to hear—he wondered how young the fellow really was. Despite the blood on his left hand, he didn't set Barrett's gut off as a dangerous person. In fact he didn't give off any signals that Barrett could read, and that felt more worrying than if he'd simply seemed violent. His calm in the face of just having murdered someone—and having been caught in the act— seemed to fit the definition of a madman all right.

"That's good, son, that's real good," Barrett said soothingly. Part of him wanted to just shoot to kill—visions of Ike's wrecked body were seared into his mind. But he'd never killed someone in cold blood when they were unarmed. He wasn't about to let this monster turn *him* into one.

Plus, there was that gut of his again— sending murky messages, but telling him loud and clear not to rush to execute this young man before he learned more about what had happened—here *and* at Ike's place.

"I don't want no more trouble either, so why don't you come with me real nice and peaceful, huh?" Barrett continued in the same calm tone.

The boy looked down at the lifeless body at his feet, then back at the sheriff. "Well, sir, reckon I still got more to do out here," he said, as if he were talking about tilling fields or chopping wood. "This ain't the only one, you know."

Barrett's stomach turned to stone. "How many more you done this to?" He pictured other sad lonely cabins like Ike's, populated only by shredded human remains and bereft pets.

The stranger pulled his sleeve up, and the sheriff saw strange black markings the length of his forearm, like pen strokes. He couldn't make out if they were letters or shapes.

"This many," the kid said.

Barrett's mind reeled. What sickness would lead a person to tally up murders they'd committed and record it on their own skin? He struggled for words. "Where?" he said finally.

"All over."

What could he mean? Barrett wasn't sure, but his first order of business had to be getting this lunatic back to town and behind bars. He'd have to deputize a few men to keep a 24-hour watch, both to ensure he stayed locked up and to prevent a lynching before the sheriff had a chance to learn more about his crimes. He hardened his tone.

"Listen to me real careful. If you don't surrender and come with me, you ain't gonna live another second." He lifted his gun a little to bring the stranger's attention to it. "You wanna stay alive, or should I end this right here and now?"

"You're makin' a mistake," the kid said with preternatural composure. "Arrestin' me won't end this."

Barrett refused to argue with him. "You comin' with me or you dyin' right here?"

A charged pause. "Comin' with you." There was a hint of sullenness, the first sign of any human reaction that Barrett could recognize. Despite everything, he felt a tinge of relief.

"You're gonna help me put this man up on the back of your horse," he told the boy, who didn't protest. Together they hauled the body, which already felt stiff, and laid it over the horse behind the saddle.

Barrett put a slipknot in a length of rope so he could quickly loop it around the kid's slender waist, and with a shorter piece he bound his hands in front of him. Then the sheriff ordered him to mount, which he did with admirable grace despite his bonds and the corpse already on there, and they returned to Ike's shack.

The old man had a horse and a mule, so they moved the body they'd brought with them to the mule and Ike's body onto his horse. Barrett felt a lump growing in his throat as they worked. The boy didn't seem much affected by the situation, but he seemed to linger by Ike, keeping his hand on him after he was already on the horse. His head was cocked slightly as if listening for something.

"Get away from him," Barrett said, his anger rising. "Mount up and let's go."

* * *

Barrett abandoned his plan of making another set of check-ins on his way back; they took the straightest route to town. Once they were in sight of the Silver Dollar and the other businesses on the outskirts, the sheriff slowed. He'd rather not parade down the main street with two mutilated corpses. He made a loop around the edge of town and approached the jail from another angle so they'd pass fewer other buildings on their way. Nonetheless, they were spotted by a few townspeople; Barrett figured they'd soon be spreading the word to others as fast as they could. Nothing he could do about that at present.

His part-time deputy was nowhere to be seen; probably loitering at the Red Rock, his favorite saloon on the other side of town from the Silver Dollar. The sheriff led his prisoner into the front office, released his hands, and directed him into one of three cells in back.

The boy went in unresisting and sat on the narrow cot. Barrett locked the door with relief. His work was just beginning, but at least the killing would stop now. Trying not to be unnerved by the young man's cool stare, he put his confiscated knife in his desk drawer and pulled out a ledger. "Now what's your name, feller?"

Silence. Barrett was afraid the man had clammed up, but he answered at last in a quiet, almost expressionless voice. "It don't matter. I ain't got nothin' to do with this no more."

"Well, it does matter for me," Barrett said. "I gotta follow the rules."

The kid set his mouth in a stubborn line. "Can you bring my rucksack in?"

"I can't let you have anything in there, son; you know that." Barrett shifted impatiently; he had so much more to do, including dealing with the dead bodies draped over horses in the shade in back of the building.

"Could you bring it in where I can see it?" Now there was an anxious edge to the kid's tone. "Please, sir."

"How about you start by tellin' me your name, and then I'll see about bringin' your things in?" Barrett was in no mood to bargain with a murderer, but he was even less inclined to waste any more time.

The boy regarded him as if assessing whether he was being honest. He apparently came to a conclusion. "Kit."

Finally. Barrett licked his pencil lead and wrote it on a blank line along with the date. "Last name?"

"Smith," Kit said. Barrett was less convinced that was his real name, but he wrote it down anyway. At least he had something for the record, and a small amount of cooperation from his prisoner.

"All right, Kit," he said.

"What about my stuff?"

"I'll get to that," Barrett said. Kit's eyes narrowed, but the sheriff turned his back on him. He wrote a few quick notes about the charges and headed outside.

"Sheriff?" His deputy Chuck, breathless, called from down the street as he came at as much of a jog as he could manage, his gray hair plastered against his forehead and temples under his shapeless hat. The former cowhand suffered from a chronic limp and a weight problem that had started once he left cattle wrangling for a less strenuous lawman position in mainly peaceful Harlan. "What's goin' on? Frank Dooley said he saw —"

"Come on," Barrett interrupted. He led the way around the side of the building, steeling himself as they rounded the corner to the back.

He explained what had happened as briefly and in as little graphic detail as possible, but the bodies of course told a fuller story. Chuck's reaction was predictable, and understandable, but Barrett had pushed his own horror to the back of his mind so he could come up with a plan.

"I need you to get Doc Simmons here," he told Chuck. "I can't be bringin' these bodies through the street." He leaned close and lowered his voice even though they were alone. "And don't be spreadin' the word that I got someone locked up for it. Don't want to get folks too stirred up before I figure out what's goin' on."

Chuck swore he wouldn't and loped back the way he'd come, panting, his limp more pronounced, which happened when he was tired. Barrett didn't doubt his good intentions but wondered if the inveterate old gossip would be able to restrain himself if townspeople started asking him what was going on.

The sheriff started back around, noticed Kit's horse from the corner of his eye, and paused long enough to hoist the rucksack off the saddle. He opened it and rummaged through it but didn't find anything of interest. An oilcloth pouch with some ancient pieces of paper tied with a ribbon nestled next to some small trinkets, a few tools and kerchiefs. He replaced the contents and slung it over his shoulder.

Kit came to the bars when he saw his bag. "Thanks, Sheriff," he said, sounding a little surprised. "Much obliged."

Barrett grunted and plopped the rucksack on his desk. He couldn't get past how unconcerned the kid seemed about what he'd done or the plight he was in. His quiet manner would've been pleasant if it weren't so jarring in contrast to what the lawman knew he'd done. But he should try to get something out of Kit while he was feeling grateful for having his bag brought in, which seemed to be the only thing his prisoner *did* care about.

He pulled his chair over to set it in front of the cell. A wave of exhaustion washed over him as he settled in it. It had been a long day already and the sun was just beginning to set. "Why don't you tell me about yourself, Kit? Where you from?"

"West," Kit said.

"And what brought you out here?"

Kit's face was inscrutable. "What you saw me doin'."

Barrett felt sick but hid it as best he could. "Can you tell me why you killed Ike Withers?"

"I don't know their names, but it ain't murder, not exactly."

The sheriff bristled. "Yeah, it is. Exactly. That old man never did no one no harm."

"Oh," Kit said. "You mean your friend in that house? I didn't kill him." He cocked his head toward the rear of the jail. "That other one likely did. That's how you found me, right? Tracking him?"

Barrett struggled to understand. "You're tryin' to tell me the man you stabbed in the head killed Old Ike?"

Kit nodded.

"And that that's why you killed him? Cause of what he done?"

Kit shrugged. "I didn't know he'd done that—but I knew what he was."

Barrett was still puzzling over the cryptic reply when Chuck came through the front door. "Sheriff, the doc's out back now."

"We'll talk more in a spell," the lawman told his prisoner.

"I ain't goin' anywhere," the kid said with a wry smile.

Shaking his head a little, Barrett went to see Doc Simmons.

The two bodies lay on the ground in the shade, the doctor crouching by them. The sheriff felt like he was really seeing them for the first time; he'd been in such a fog of horror and so focused on getting them transported and the killer safely locked away that maybe he hadn't really studied them closely. He realized the two corpses looked very different from one another.

"Hell of a thing," Doc Simmons said hoarsely.

Barrett nodded grimly. "What can you tell me, Beth?"

She straightened, dusted her skirt off absentmindedly, and looked down at the cadavers. "Poor Ike. Something chewed his face clean off, even got to his brain. Ate a good deal of his guts too. Coyotes?"

"I don't think so," Barrett said reluctantly. "You think—a man could do that to another man?"

She exhaled low, almost a whistle. "I don't know. You hear things, right?" She didn't say, but the sheriff imagined she was thinking about the Donner party. That'd been about twenty years back and hundreds of miles away, but the stories he'd heard about it still haunted his imagination and many others', he guessed. But even in their desperate state, they hadn't done anything like this—attacking another living thing and devouring them like a wild animal would.

"What about the other one?" Barrett asked. The other dead man was a stranger to him, a short, slight man in his thirties, from what he could tell.

The doctor shook her head. "I can't figure this one out." She knelt next to him, grimacing at his odor as she got close. The sheriff could smell it even from where he was, and it was unlike that of any recently deceased body he'd ever encountered. It reminded him of the dark, almost spicy stench of a long-dead, decomposing animal.

"He didn't die from this stab wound," Simmons said, pointing to the top of the corpse's head where Barrett had seen Kit drive his knife. "That happened sometime after he was dead—there's no real bleeding. The only thing I can think of—" she pulled the dead man's shirt off his left shoulder, revealing a ragged hole where a chunk of flesh had been torn off "—is maybe he was attacked by an animal and got infected." She pulled out a hanky and wiped her hands, though they weren't visibly soiled. "He's been dead at least a few days, maybe a week or more."

* * *

Barrett sent Chuck to fetch dinner for Kit from the nearby Keystone Cafe—with another warning to keep everything under wraps a little longer—after the two men dragged the bodies into the jail's stable. The Keystone served plain, bland food but gave the lawmen a steep discount and an account they settled monthly. The sheriff opted to return to the Silver Dollar for his meal.

Anneleigh was there already, finishing a piece of apple pie, when he entered. His heart skipped a beat, and he thought longingly back to earlier in the day, when his night had looked much more promising.

"Evening, Miss Klein," he said, tipping his hat as she looked up. "All right if I join you?"

"Certainly, Sheriff," she said graciously, but with a little twinkle in her eye that did something funny to his insides. He sat down; Billy would bring him dinner without having to order when he had a chance. Anneleigh's sweet floral orange scent drifted across the small table to him, and he was suddenly self-conscious, remembering that he'd never gotten a chance to wash off the sweat and trail dust. He hadn't even been home to put on a clean shirt. But if the lady noticed or minded, she gave no indication.

Anneleigh sipped her coffee and dabbed the sides of her mouth with a handkerchief, wiping away a few crumbs of pie crust. She could put away alcohol almost as well as any man, but only when she was at the bar of the social club. She did wear lipstick and rouge when out and about, which earned her some disapproving looks from the proper ladies in town, but her manners and behavior were impeccable, and her hair was always neatly pulled up and pinned under a hat. In public, that is.

"What's this I hear about some trouble outside of town?" Anneleigh asked. "Is it true someone's been killed?"

Barrett sighed, tantalizing memories dissipating from his mind. "Yes'm. I can't talk about it yet, though. Still workin' it all out myself."

"What happened to the fellow who warned about the madman?" That part of the story at least appeared to have spread, but it wasn't surprising considering the number of townspeople who'd witnessed it firsthand.

"I don't know," he replied, lost in thought. He suddenly felt foolish for not having looked for the witness earlier. Then again, it wasn't like he'd been sitting around twiddling his thumbs all afternoon and evening. Besides, having seen the kid murder someone firsthand—a much more serious crime than the alleged attack on Wally—he hadn't been thinking he needed another witness. "I need to find him though. Something about this ain't right."

Billy brought his food—meat pie; apparently he was inclined toward making pastry today—and Barrett looked at it, his appetite replaced by a nagging feeling that he needed to find Wally. Nevertheless he ate to keep up his strength. Anneleigh excused herself; business would just be picking up at the club. He had a feeling she would've made time for him that night, but he wasn't sure when he'd be done chasing information about the murders, so he didn't ask. He watched her leave regretfully, then turned his attention to devouring his dinner as quickly as he could.

* * *

His wandering reconnoiter of the few streets that had businesses open into the night was fruitless, as was his questioning of all the innkeepers in town. Wally hadn't bought a room for the night anywhere, and he wasn't spinning his wild yarns at any of the bars (or the social club, which Barrett checked first). Accosting passers-by to see if they'd seen him didn't help either. It wasn't until the thirteen-year-old son of Burt McKay—the apothecary whose shop and home shared a wall with Doc Simmons's office—tracked Barrett down on the street that he learned the whereabouts of the stranger.

He followed the kid to the doctor's office. Simmons let him in and led him to her examining room, where Wally lay upon a small hard cot. "What happened, Beth?"

Simmons placed a folded wet strip of cloth on Wally's forehead. "He was found delirious on the street about half an hour ago," she said. "He fainted away almost as soon as they brought him here." She pulled up his right sleeve to reveal a white bandage stained with red covering most of his forearm. Unfastening it, she gently lifted it away.

The ragged wound he'd claimed was made by a man biting him had festered as if an infection had been spreading for days or weeks, yet it had only been a few hours since Barrett had seen it last. "He said he just got this today," Barrett finally said. "Have you ever seen anything rot this fast, Beth?"

"Sure ain't, Sheriff," she said grimly.

"Can you make him come to?"

"I've tried. He's dead to the world."

"Damn." Barrett shook his head. "I needed this feller to explain what the hell is going on. I can't make heads nor tails of it." He closed his eyes, thinking, then opened them and fixed his stare on Simmons. "Doc, you're smarter than me and Chuck put together. You got to help me."

She seemed to be directing her full attention on the task of redressing Wally's wound. But she nodded slowly without looking up. "I'll try. Why don't you tell me everything you've been holding back about this mess?"

* * *

Simmons returned to the jail once she got Burt to say he'd check in on her patient occasionally until she got back.

"He really looks like he's been dead a while," she said, re-examining the stranger's corpse by lantern light on the straw-covered floor of the stable. "You're sure you saw him struggling with your prisoner?"

Barrett ran back through what he'd seen. He'd been hot and tired, the Nevada sun still high in the sky, with the ghastly discovery of Ike's body fresh in his mind. And yet. "Yeah," he said with certainty. "I didn't get a clear view of everything that was happenin', but I know I saw him strugglin' until the kid put a knife in his head."

Simmons laughed disbelievingly. "Then everything I thought I knew about bodies was wrong," she said. "And this boy Kit claims this is the fellow who killed Ike?"

It was Barrett's turn to scoff. "Yeah," he said. "Which if he was already dead, ain't possible either."

She turned to Ike's body. "I don't know. He was old but he still had a lot of strength. Hard to believe either of those scrawny men overpowered him, if your prisoner is the same build as that fellow like you say." She leaned closer to Ike. "I mean, without him putting up a fight ..." She touched one of Ike's hands, turning it over, then straightened suddenly. "He did fight back," she said.

"How do you know?"

"He's got somebody's skin under his fingernails." Now she was bending over the other corpse. "It's hard to tell with this body in the state it is, but these could be scratch marks."

* * *

"You must be Kit," the doctor said. "How do you do. I'm Dr. Simmons."

"Evenin', Doc," Kit said in his soft voice.

"Now, Kit," Barrett said, "we need you to do everything the doc says. It's real important."

"Yes sir," Kit said, calm and docile as ever.

"I'm gonna have you undress, Kit, so I can examine you," Simmons said.

The boy looked startled, the biggest reaction he'd had to anything that had happened yet. "Ma'am?"

"It'll just be through the bars, but I need to see every inch of your skin," Simmons said firmly. "You needn't feel ashamed or worry about my modesty, young man; I'm a doctor."

Kit was already shaking his head slightly before she finished. He looked out at the lawmen and back at her. "Don't reckon I want to do that," he said mildly but with a stubborn edge to his voice.

"Kit," Barrett said sternly. He cast about for an idea of how to carry this off without force. "You want to keep your rucksack, you ought to do as the doc says."

Kit's eyes widened, then his brows came down over them. The others waited tensely for his answer. He turned his gaze back to Simmons.

"Please, Doc, not in front of everyone? I'll do it if you make them leave."

"Hm." She looked at Barrett. "What do you think, Sheriff? Can I trust these bars to protect me if you and Chuck leave me alone with him?"

Barrett didn't like it, but nor did he relish the thought of taking the young man's clothes off by force. "Yeah, they'll hold. We'll be right

53

outside with the door cocked open, so give a holler if he tries any funny business and we'll be back in the blink of an eye." He pointed warningly at Kit. "So if you don't want to strip down in front of us, or get shot, you behave for the doc."

He and Chuck waited just outside, silent so they could listen for any signs of trouble inside. Luckily they were far enough away from the nightlife that the street was empty and quiet. Other than some unintelligible but calm conversation between Kit and Simmons, it sounded uneventful inside the jail as well.

Simmons soon emerged, shutting the door behind her. Her face was serious and thoughtful. "No scratches anywhere," she said. "A few bruises and those odd markings on his arm, but I don't believe he could've been the one who killed Ike."

Barrett exhaled in a loud gust. He was frustrated and confused but also felt an edge of relief—which was even more confusing. "So maybe that other feller really did do it, and our friend in there is a hero." He was unconvinced even as he said it. "We'll hold onto him a while longer. Here's hopin' Wally comes to and can point his finger at one of 'em as the man that bit him—that'd clear this up real quick." He smoothed his mustache down with the thumb and forefinger of his left hand as he thought. "'Til then—"

A distant cry, carried clear to their ears on the silent street, stopped him mid-sentence. It was a terrible sound, full of shock and pain. All three of them turned in the direction of it. No movement was detected, though it was hard to see very far; lights of any kind were few and far between in this quiet part of town.

Another cry sounded and Barrett bolted toward it. "Stay here, Beth!" he shouted over his shoulder. "Chuck, let's go!" He didn't pause to see if his deputy followed. He pelted down the uneven, wagon-wheel-rutted street as fast as he could in the near-darkness.

He followed the sound of more cries, though they seemed to be getting weaker even as they sounded closer. Then he saw some sort of commotion on the wooden walkway to their left, about ten yards ahead.

His gut churned. Whatever was going on, it was happening right outside Doc Simmons's office and the apothecary.

Barrett drew his gun and jogged forward, though more cautiously. He was now close enough to see two men grappling on the ground. "You there!" he shouted. "Get away from each other! Hands up where I can see 'em—now!"

One was clearly being bested by the other, his arms flailing weakly and erratically in their attempt to fend off his assailant. The other lifted his head at the sound of Barrett's voice, still pinning the man under him but staring toward the sheriff.

Barrett didn't like the way his head had swiveled. It didn't look natural or exactly *human*. He didn't like the face he could now make out in the dim glow from a nearby house window, either.

The man's eyes were clouded in the way he'd seen them become on dead bodies. At first in the shadows it looked as if part of his lower jaw were missing. Then Barrett realized it was just much darker than the rest of his face. And he realized what the chin was coated with—dripping with—that made it appear so much darker.

"Get off him." His own voice sounded weak and breathless, as if he'd just been punched in the gut. His shaking hands raised his gun.

He didn't have to ask twice. The man launched himself from the ground, his movements fast but clumsy and erratic as he lunged toward the sheriff.

Barrett fired when the assailant was about five feet away, and kept firing, hitting him square in the chest and stomach at least four times. The man kept running, and Barrett heard his empty cylinder click. He threw his gun aside, lowered his head, and rammed his shoulder into the man's chest, sending him flying.

Barrett pounced before the attacker had a chance to get up. He pressed the man facedown into the pavement and knelt on him to keep him there while he forced one wrist and then the other into handcuffs. It wasn't easy. The man writhed with an unnatural strength despite several visible exit wounds in his back where the sheriff's bullets had gone clean through him. His arms were stiff and hard to bend behind his back.

At last the sheriff had him cuffed, and he tied the man's ankles with a length of rawhide for good measure. The man whipped around wildly but couldn't roll over or get very far on the ground, let alone stand.

"Sheriff!" Barrett turned his attention to Chuck, who was kneeling over the other man. "It's Burt McKay. I think he's … dead."

The lawman hurried over. It was easy to confirm both. The apothecary hadn't been savaged to the extent that Ike had—possibly because the killer had been interrupted—but he was undeniably dead, his entrails pulled partly out through a hole in his abdomen, his throat ripped open, a pool of blood slowly spreading under his head and shoulders.

Despite his horror, Barrett realized he definitely had the murderer in custody this time. He left Chuck sitting helplessly by Burt's body and returned his attention to the man he'd cuffed and tied.

Keeping a foot or two of distance between him and his writhing, growling prisoner, he bent to see his face. When the sheriff's own face came into the man's view, he paused in his frantic movements and snarled in a way that Barrett had never heard from a human or an animal. His teeth snapped together as he bit the air, staring straight at Barrett (though with his pale murky eyes, it was hard to tell what, if anything, he saw).

It took the sheriff a few moments to get past the horror of the man's waxy-looking skin, blank gaze, and gnashing teeth and realize who he was looking at.

"Wally!" he burst out. Chuck looked over. "It's Wally—the feller that got bit, that Doc was takin' care of."

Chuck started to stand, then stumbled and fell. He looked back, confused, and tried to get up again, but something dragged him down.

It was Burt's hand, clamped onto his belt. As Barrett watched in shock, the apothecary's body spasmed and then moved to a sitting position in a jerky, halting set of movements. He was reminded of a puppet—one whose strings were being controlled by an amateur puppeteer.

Then Burt wasn't moving slowly anymore. He surged to life and grabbed Chuck by the neck. His head darted toward him and, before Barrett could even make a move toward him, tore off the deputy's nose with his teeth.

Blood spurted and Barrett heard himself let out a horrified sound he'd never made before as Chuck screamed in a muffled, distorted way and fell to the ground. The sheriff scrambled to his feet, fumbling for his gun before remembering it was lying empty of bullets a few feet away in the street.

He came up behind Burt, who was now on top of Chuck in much the same way Wally had pinned *him* down, and grabbed his shoulders. Burt didn't look up from his gruesome work on Chuck's face until Barrett yanked him back with all his strength. He and Burt tumbled and landed on their backs close together and, before the sheriff could right himself, the apothecary (or the thing that he'd become) pounced.

Barrett felt frantic. All he could focus on was that blood-stained mouth, twisted and gaping and biting at the air. The lawman held the monster at arm's length, and the Burt-thing twisted its head from side to side, snapping and trying to latch onto Barrett's hands.

Suddenly Burt's mouth distorted even more. Barrett realized a shot had rung out, and some of Burt's teeth and part of his jaw had disintegrated into a red mess. It only stopped his attack for a few seconds—he was knocked off balance momentarily but didn't appear to feel any pain—but it was enough for Barrett to throw him off and stand up. Burt swayed unsteadily by the door to Doc Simmons's office, and Barrett ran at him, shoving him inside and pulling the door closed.

"Step aside!" He looked back, surprised, and saw the doctor herself standing there. In one hand she held a four-barrel derringer, in the other a key. He moved away and she locked the door just as it started to rattle.

"That won't hold for long," she told Barrett. He looked around for something to barricade it with, but his eyes fell on his deputy. Chuck lay on the ground, clutching his destroyed face, choking and whimpering in a way that made every nerve ending in the sheriff's body ache with empathy. There was too much to do. He ran to Chuck and tried to shove him over but the older man groaned and batted his hand away.

"You gotta roll onto your side," Barrett said into his ear. "Otherwise you're gonna drown in your own blood." He felt like crying, something he hadn't done since his wife had died. Chuck seemed to understand and shifted himself little by little, never taking his hands from his face or ceasing his pitiful wailing.

"Sheriff!" Simmons's voice cut sharply through the fog in his head. He pivoted and saw the door to her office was shaking as if Burt were hurling himself against it repeatedly. "Take him out with my gun when he gets through," she said, holding out the small pistol.

Barrett looked back at Wally, still hissing and struggling against his bonds as energetically as before, despite having been shot several times.

"He ain't gonna die," the sheriff muttered.

"What?" she said in that same sharp tone, her voice remarkably not shaking like his was.

"Look at Wally!" he shouted. "He won't die no matter how much I shoot him! Burt's sick like him—he won't die neither."

Simmons nodded and pocketed her gun, eyes scanning the street. "In here!" She pushed her way into the apothecary, the door of which sat ajar—Burt must've left it open when he went to check on Wally, Barrett had time to think as he followed her.

"Help me get this barrel against my door," the doctor panted. She wasn't a weak woman, but the barrel didn't budge when she threw her weight against it.

Barrett forced his legs to move, and he grabbed the other side. Together, they could lift it for brief moments, drag it across the floor at others. For what felt like an eternity they strained and grunted and inched it out the door of the apothecary.

They pushed it against the doctor's front door none too soon — they could see the wood starting to buckle, its hinges failing. But the barrel stopped it from moving any farther.

"What now?" Barrett whispered. He might ordinarily have felt ashamed of depending entirely on Doc Simmons to do the thinking when it was his job to protect the town, but he felt his mind collapsing under the weight of everything that had happened that day, just like how the doc's door was slowly being battered down.

"That should hold him for a while," Simmons said. "And Wally isn't going anywhere. What about Chuck? Will this happen to him too?"

Chuck. Barrett had blocked out what was happening to his deputy while he threw everything he had into moving that barrel. They approached him cautiously; a pool of blood had spread from his destroyed face, and he wasn't moving or moaning any more. A faint labored gurgle could be heard when they crouched by him.

Simmons felt his wrist, touched his chest, studied his face, and shook her head. "I can't fix this," she said regretfully. "He doesn't have long, and he's suffering something awful." She produced her derringer from her skirt pocket. "Should I—?"

"Oh Lord," Barrett said mournfully. "I—I don't know. And I don't know—what'd happen next if you—if he—"

"Right," she breathed. "Well then." She pocketed the gun, took off her hat, which had been hanging askew, and threw it aside. Half the pins in her hair had come loose and some of it fell around her face and down her back in loose locks, but she didn't seem to notice.

"Here's what we're going to do, Sheriff," she said firmly. "You're going back to the jail. You're going to get that—boy, Kit. You're going to ask him what we should do."

"What?" Barrett blinked, dazed and uncomprehending.

"Don't make me slap you, Sheriff," Simmons said severely. "Kit knows what to do. That's what he was doing when you came across him. You need him. *We* need him."

That made some sense, or else Barrett was just clinging desperately to the hope that something would, eventually. "What about him?" he asked, nodding toward Chuck, although he couldn't bear to look at him or say his name.

"I'll stay with Chuck," Simmons said. "I can't do anything for him, but he oughtn't have to be alone right now." She raised her hand almost before the sheriff could begin to protest. "I have my gun if anything happens."

"And what if that don't work?" Barrett asked.

"Then I will run," she said with finality. "I'll come to you and—Kit'll help us stop him somehow. Now *go!*"

The sheriff took off at a clumsy lope, stumbling several times. His ability to dodge the wheel ruts and rocks of the street seemed to have deserted him. But he didn't fall, and he made it back to the jail. Along the way, some of his wits returned to him.

He burst into the building. The boy was lying on his prison cot—even smaller and harder than the one in Doc's office—staring at the ceiling.

"You there!" Barrett said with all the sternness he could muster. "Get up."

Kit turned his head but otherwise didn't move. His large dark eyes regarded the sheriff coolly. "Why?"

"Because you brought this poison into my town, and you need to stop it." Barrett surprised himself with that bitter outburst—he hadn't known that was what he was going to say.

The young man looked away again. "Way I recall it, *you* forced *me* to stop fightin' it like I wanted to."

Barrett was apoplectic for a moment, rage welling up like a flooded creek reaching the top of its banks. Then his anger deflated just as suddenly. "My deputy is gone," he said, his voice breaking. "Poor old Chuck. Unless—" he gave voice to his terrible dread "—unless he's *not* gone." Kit was watching him again, unreadable. "Please, kid," Barrett said. "You gotta help me. You know about these—this sickness. Right?" He continued desperately in the face of the prisoner's obstinate silence. "I'll set you free. I'll pay you a reward. I'll do anything—please. This is my town, and I'm s'posed to protect 'em, and I—I—I let 'em all down."

He took the keys down from the wall with shaking hands and unlocked the cell, pushed it open, stood aside. "Please, kid, please," he said hoarsely.

Kit stood fluidly, looking small and slight, and the sheriff wondered how much he'd really be able to help, even if he agreed to. But Barrett had no other ideas, nothing left in his spent brain and body.

"I need my knife," Kit said.

"Whatever you say," Barrett said, suddenly aware of time passing. "Let's hurry—I left the doc alone with—with—" he almost said "one of them" until he remembered it was Chuck, mortally wounded but still Chuck, and he trailed off instead.

Kit wasn't stopping to listen anyway. He went to the sheriff's desk with quick, light steps and opened the drawer. He'd apparently noted where Barrett had stashed the weapon.

The lawman had an awful moment where he thought the kid would gut him and take off, leaving him to bleed out and his town doctor to die by the hands of his deputy. But Kit just gripped his knife at his side and dashed out of the jail with the sheriff in tow.

"That way," Barrett said, and they ran, Kit easily outpacing him, in the direction of the doctor's office and apothecary.

Kit reached Wally first; his strenuous flailing had enabled the man or creature or whatever it was to travel several feet down the dusty street, but still on his stomach, still cuffed and bound, so he could only inch along.

The boy crouched next to him, so close the sheriff wanted to shout a warning, and Wally raised his head. Barrett could hear the inhuman snarling and hissing coming out of the thing.

Kit raised his knife in the air, holding it with both hands, and drove it straight down into Wally's skull. The terrible sounds stopped immediately. Kit sat for several seconds next to him, hand on Wally's shoulder, eyes closed, until Simmons, who had been watching from her spot next to Chuck, used her sharp voice. "Young man, we've got a few more problems over here."

Kit took one more second and then opened his eyes. He joined her by Chuck's side.

"He's dead," Simmons said, giving Barrett a pitying look. "It happened just a moment ago. Is he going to—turn?"

The kid knelt and made the same gesture he had with Wally, resting his hand on Chuck's shoulder, head bent and eyes closed as if in prayer.

"No," he said to the doctor. "He's gone." Without further explanation, he made his way to the office door that still shuddered even though it was solidly blocked by the barrel. "Is there another way in?" he asked Simmons.

"That's the only one," she said. "The windows are too small to get through."

Kit looked consideringly at one of them. "Tight fit I reckon," he agreed. "All right, pull the barrel away then."

Reluctantly, Barrett and Simmons threw their weight into moving the protective barrier while Kit stood at the ready. The door banged halfway open and the doctor gave a little shriek of surprise—the first time she'd really lost her composure—as Burt's arm and head came through the opening, hand flailing, reaching blindly for something to grip, teeth bared in a demonic snarl that seemed all too familiar by now.

Kit stepped close, raised his knife and lodged it deep in the man's head. Again the noise stopped almost immediately, and again he touched the creature's shoulder as if communing with it for a brief spell.

"Is it over?" Now there was a detectable quiver in Doc Simmons's voice.

"Yes, Beth," Barrett breathed. "It's over."

"No it ain't." They turned to Kit. He was wiping his knife on the sleeve covering Burt's one arm that had made it through the door.

"Who else?" Barrett's heart sank. "Ike?"

"Naw," Kit said. "He ain't coming back. But there's bound to be others."

"He could be right," Simmons said suddenly. "The men who brought Wally to me said he'd been delirious, acting half mad. Fighting, I think they said."

"Biting, maybe." Barrett said it. They both looked at him. "That's what does it, right? Like rabies?"

"More or less," Kit said after a brief pause.

"Where'd they grab him from?" Barrett asked Simmons. "Did they say?"

She searched her memory for a few seconds. "I believe they said he'd gotten kicked out of the social club."

Barrett's insides turned to ice.

* * *

The lights and noise of the saloons drew closer as Kit and Barrett rode through town. Doc Simmons had been convinced to stay behind to take care of Burt's newly widowed wife and son, who'd been cowering in the quarters above the apothecary, too terrified by the sounds below to come out until the struggle was over.

At the Silver Dollar, just across the street from the social club, a piano tinkled and men's voices roared jovially, with peals of women's laughter occasionally carrying above the rest of the hubbub.

The brothel itself—a fairly well-built structure with a Victorian facade—was always far less boisterous, and tonight was no exception. A lantern with red glass panes glowed by the door, the only indication that it was anything other than a genteel home.

The hastily discussed plan had been to gather reinforcements from the saloon if trouble was evident, but it seemed quiet. Raising the alarm to a roomful of drunk, rowdy men seemed like an unnecessary risk.

They dismounted and went up the step to the front porch with Barrett in the lead. His knock brought Belle Watkins, the proprietress.

"Why, Sheriff," she said with a smile and eyebrows raised. "Comin' to the front door for a second time tonight—what a surprise."

Barrett felt his face grow a little warm, even though discretion was the least of his problems right now. He'd arranged with her to let him enter through the rear entrance when he visited, thinking it would be easier for the proper part of Harlan society to tolerate his patronage of the establishment if he was less blatant about it. It also bothered him that the revelers of the nightlife district would assume he was taking liberties in exchange for protecting the business, as he knew some lawmen did in other towns. He never even accepted a discount, but no one would've believed it.

"And who's your handsome young friend?" Belle continued as if she didn't notice his embarrassment. "I don't believe we've had the pleasure." She extended her hand to Kit, who took it after a hesitation and introduced himself softly.

"Belle, I'm here on official business," Barrett said, finding his voice at last. "This here—this here's Kit. I've deputized him for the night."

"Oh?" she said. "Where's Deputy Arnold? Got the night off?"

The sheriff pushed aside the crushing wave of sorrow that hit him. "Chuck's—well, he's—" he shook his head. "I'll explain later. Right now we need to take a look around the club, see if there's been any trouble."

"Why would there be—?"

"Please, Belle," Barrett said with growing impatience. "I ain't got time for niceties. Just let me in."

Her lips tightened a little at the uncharacteristic brusqueness, but she stepped aside and let them in.

In the main drawing room, a handful of women sat demurely on sofas and chairs, some holding teacups that could contain either whiskey or actual tea. Another was playing a soft, slow melody on a piano in the corner. Their heavy makeup and white dresses gave them away for what they were, but not their prim poise. A couple of them had men sitting next to them, hats in hand, one looking awkward and ill at ease, another more confident and comfortable. Everyone looked up when the sheriff came into the center of the room.

"I need everyone's attention," he said unnecessarily. "Have any of you been in a tussle with someone actin' odd? Anyone been bit?"

The confused looks told him they hadn't. A few even laughed with surprise at the idea.

"All right," he said. He turned back to Belle. "You seen anything like that?"

She looked a little startled. "Earlier this evenin', shortly after the first time you checked in with us as a matter of fact, I had to have Clyde throw someone out who'd had too much to drink, or worse—possibly opium. One of our patrons claimed he'd bit him, and sure enough, he did the same to Clyde as he was escorting him to the door."

"Why didn't you report it?"

Belle laughed a little. "Well, Sheriff, it was unusual, but it certainly wasn't serious enough to bring the law into it. You know opium fiends can go a little mad. And we rid ourselves of him before he caused too much trouble. No one was badly hurt."

"What happened to the fellers that were bit?" Kit's soft voice interjected.

"Clyde is resting in the back room with a headache," Belle said. "He said to call for him if I needed him. The other gentleman is upstairs; he paid for a full night, so he may be asleep by now."

Barrett and Kit exchanged a glance. "You check on Clyde—but be careful, he's a big man," the sheriff said in a low voice. "Miss Belle, I'm gonna need you to show me where the other feller is."

"Sheriff, this is quite—" She saw the look on his face and sighed. "Very well. Come with me."

He followed her up the stairs, his hand not on the butt of his gun but lightly gripping the handle of a Bowie knife he'd strapped to his waist.

Though telltale sounds of lovemaking came through some of the closed doors they passed, it was nearly as quiet upstairs as it had been on the main floor. Belle stopped at the last door on the right and, looking reluctant, rapped lightly. "Mister?" After a pause, she knocked again. "Excuse me, sir, may we speak to you for a moment?"

This time there was some movement heard on the other side of the door. A sort of rustling, and then the door rattled a little. The bumping grew louder and more urgent; the door shuddered against someone's insistent, repeated shoves.

Belle looked confused. "Just turn the doorknob, Mister," she called. She reached for the handle on her side. Barrett protested and started to reach his hand out to stop her, feeling as if everything was happening slow, like in a dream, but it was too late. Belle turned the knob and pushed the door open a little. At first she appeared to face some resistance, but then it swung inward with a sudden jerking movement.

A man burst out into the hall. Belle was propelled backward and they crashed into the wall together.

Barrett's dreamlike state dissipated with the suddenness of the attack. He grabbed the man, skinny and gray-haired but surprisingly strong and stubborn, and pulled him off Belle, losing his balance with the force he had to use to get him to move. Barrett fell heavily onto the wooden floor, bringing the man down with him.

The man twisted and flailed frantically, rolling off Barrett in a chaotic way. The sheriff had lost his grip on his knife, but he found it still in its sheath and yanked it out. He stumbled up onto his knees and stabbed downward at the man's head. His first attempt went wild and hit his neck. Blood flowed, but not as copious as Barrett would've expected. He pulled his blade out and drove it down again, this time through the left eye socket. It penetrated the man's head and stopped its slide suddenly, as if the tip had pierced the inner back wall of the skull. He struggled frantically to dislodge it, but he realized the body under him was now unmoving. Feeling calmer, he braced one hand against the man's forehead and yanked the knife out.

A scream behind him brought him to his feet. He pushed past Belle, who was leaning against the wall in shock, and hurried into the bedroom the man had come from.

Anneleigh looked up, the dark makeup around her teary eyes smudged and running. She was sitting on the edge of the bed, holding the hand of a pale, slender ginger-haired figure wearing a white nightgown mottled with dark stains. With a pang in his heart he recognized the girl, with whom he'd had a couple of sweet encounters on nights when Anneleigh was unavailable and he'd felt too lonely and hungry to wait another day. "Penny's hurt," she said in a low, shaking voice. "I think she's—"

Barrett grabbed her and pulled her away roughly.

"What're you doing, John?" Anneleigh cried. "Penny needs me!" She struggled against him.

He felt awful but held fast, dragging her toward the door. She broke away and returned to her friend's side.

"Annie, please," Barrett said, gripping her shoulder, "get away from her. Penny ain't well. She might—"

Penny's eyes opened. Anneleigh didn't notice at first; she'd twisted around to face Barrett, looking like she was about to argue. He saw, however. With more force this time, he grabbed Anneleigh. She struggled against him again at first, then went still as she saw the red-haired girl rise from the bed, her movements strangely stiff but spasmodic, like a faulty machine.

Barrett put himself between Anneleigh and the thing that used to be Penny. The girl flung herself toward him, so suddenly that he barely got his hands up to hold her back, her teeth snapping inches from his face, her eyes like milky blue marbles rolling in their sockets. "Annie," he panted, "where's my knife? I think I dropped it in the hall."

He couldn't look back to see Anneleigh and she didn't reply. He was able to hold Penny at bay, but she was so wild and unpredictable that it took all his focus. He dropped one hand briefly to slap at his sheath and confirm the knife was gone, then brought it back up to grab onto the writhing woman hissing and growling and fighting unceasingly to get to him.

He felt something at his shoulder and jumped, pivoting around in a kind of ghoulish parody of a dance with Penny, expecting to see another monster. It was Anneleigh, black-rimmed eyes wide, holding up his knife.

He gusted relief. Shifting his grip so one hand was around the creature's willowy neck, he reached out with the other one and Anneleigh put the knife within reach. He made sure he had a firm grip on it and took careful aim—he didn't want to stab what had been a quiet, charming girl more than he had to. As she bent her head down to try and bite the arm that held her back, he drove the knife down as hard as he could through the top of her skull. It cracked through the bone and he buried it up to the hilt.

Penny sagged and dropped to the floor with his knife lodged in her. He covered his face, panting, and started to cry.

A soft hand touched his, pulling his fingers away from his eyes. Anneleigh drew him into her arms and he clung to her like a drowning man.

There was a commotion downstairs and he, Belle, and Anneleigh raced to the top of the stairs, looking down. Kit strode into view and stood at the bottom landing, knife held casually at his side. "I got mine," he said. "How about you?"

* * *

The sheriff quickly pulled himself together, or managed to pretend to, and he and Kit made the rounds upstairs. The occupants of the other bedrooms had come into the hall or were peering out from behind their doors, so it was easy to verify that no one else had been bitten.

He found and deputized several men he knew to be reliable (and who weren't too drunk) to help him and Kit ride through the town, rousing the citizens, warning them of the danger, and directing them to the main street, the widest, best-tended thoroughfare in Harlan.

Barrett looked out at the sea of lanterns and tired, frightened faces, and explained the threat facing them as best he could, based on what he'd experienced and what little additional information Kit had imparted. He told them how to spot a potential threat and also the importance of the deep head wound to neutralize attackers.

Flanked by Doc Simmons and Belle Watkins, he had his wild, nearly inconceivable story verified by two of the most trusted citizens in their respective sides of the town.

Then he sought volunteers to help carry the bodies of friends and neighbors turned monsters (except Chuck, who inexplicably hadn't turned when he died) to the undertaker's, where they were lined up in a sad, gruesome row on his floor.

After securing promises from his new temporary deputies that they'd help him make the rounds of more outlying homesteads in the area in the morning, Barrett let everyone return to their homes.

By the time he'd dispersed everyone, hopefully armed with enough knowledge to be prepared for whatever might be coming next, Kit and his horse were nowhere to be found. Barrett returned to the jail; the kid's rucksack was gone as well.

"John." He turned to see Anneleigh in the doorway.

"Annie." He was too tired to feel self-conscious about using his favorite nickname for her, but not too tired to feel a swelling of love and longing at her silhouette in the doorway. "I'm sorry about … everything."

She moved inside and he could see her clearly; she'd wiped away some of her smeared makeup but still looked disheveled. Somehow she was more beautiful than ever. "You saved so many folks tonight, honey," she said. "You did so good."

Barrett burst into tears for the second time that night—and only the second time in over a decade. And for the second time, Anneleigh came to him and held him tight.

The time for propriety and bashfulness was over. "Annie, stay with me tonight," he pleaded into her ear. "Stay with me for good."

2: ROSALIE

The goats were feeling frisky in the warm afternoon. Rosalie's favorite, Prudence, loped up the steep grassy slope at the base of James Peak, and the girl followed her at a slower pace, panting a little by the time she caught up to where the goat had found a patch of shrubs she deemed suitable for grazing.

Instead of sitting next to her as she often would, Rosalie stood and looked up at the mountain. The grass was already patchy where she and Prudence had stopped, and it wasn't too far above them that it gave way to great swaths of rock and groves of evergreens.

She tried to picture what it would be like to scale it. The deep crevices in the rock, sharp drop-offs partly obscured by pine trees, seemed treacherous. She wondered what the other side of the mountain was like. Maybe it just plunged straight down, a sheer impassible cliff face.

Rosalie turned and looked down the slope at the little village of Yancy, the only home she'd ever known, nestled between two mountains, James Peak and Mount Payne. The only way they ever got visitors was if they turned off from the wagon road that skirted the valley about a mile away. A faint path led from that road to her village, but travelers not looking for it rarely noticed it. Now it had been obscured with brush so it was even less detectable.

We are the chosen ones. She tried out the words in her head, but they felt flat, unconvincing. *We are the trapped ones.* That rang much more true.

The sun had gone behind some gray clouds in the few minutes she'd been standing there.

She rested her crook on her arm and loosened the ribbons of her bonnet, retying them loosely so it could fall behind her and rest lightly on her back. The gathering breeze disheveled her hair, but it seemed to help clear her mind. As she stared at Yancy, at the small figures moving here and there like pieces on a checkerboard, an idea began to take shape.

A tinkling sound diverted her attention from the village and her thoughts. Off to her left and down a ways, the brush grew more thickly. A bell had been tied to a bush within the thicket, one of many scattered throughout the area surrounding Yancy. They'd been placed in recent months and were meant to raise an alert in case anyone (or anything) intruded into their valley, but the only time Rosalie ever heard them ring was when one of her goats triggered them by digging into a bramble looking for tasty leaves.

She walked unhurriedly in the direction of the sound, doing a mental count of her goats as she went. Besides Prudence there were eight others. When a dip in the terrain came into view, she spotted the horns and ears of the ninth goat, an older billy she called Grimm. He preferred to graze lower on the slope; his climbing days were mostly over.

She gave a little nod as she completed her count. She was almost to the bush before her distracted mind rang a warning bell of its own; if all nine goats were accounted for, then what had triggered the alarm?

She had exactly enough time to formulate that thought before the bell rang again, hectically, and someone burst from the bushes at her.

Rosalie stumbled backward, feet tangling in tough, scratchy weeds, and fell heavily on her back. She nearly lost hold of her crook but tightened her grip, squeezing it with panicky strength as she brought it in front of her, putting her other hand on the base and holding it out like a barrier against her attacker as he pounced.

Her arms nearly buckled under the force of the man's onslaught as he threw his full weight on her with a chaotic abandon that somehow didn't seem human. There was something wrong with his face, too. She strained to hold him at bay, her fear giving her added strength as she stared into eyes that were opaque and milky, like a sky full of clouds, and at jaws that snapped like those of an attack dog.

Keeping him at arm's length took all of her attention, so she couldn't focus on finding a way out of this predicament. All she could do was press upward as her muscles burned and began to weaken, staring at the snarling, inhuman face.

It took only seconds to recognize him, but it seemed an eternity before she fully grasped who it was. Her surprise broke her concentration for a moment, and she faltered, letting him get a few inches closer. He responded with a renewed ferocity, straining to reach her, gnashing his teeth. His clumsy arms flailed at her, and this time one of his hands caught in her hair, pulling painfully. Rosalie screamed.

The man's skull split without warning, and his terrible face froze in mid-growl. He sagged against the crook, and the sudden change was all it took to collapse Rosalie's quickly weakening muscles. The body on top of her felt cold and stiff, and its pungent odor—of dirt and minerals and rotting flesh—overwhelmed her senses. She struggled wildly but ineffectually under its weight, not recognizing the inarticulate moans she heard as her own voice.

The pressure on her chest and stomach eased suddenly. The body rose up, and she briefly thought the man wasn't really dead and was launching another attack. Then she saw someone else's hands hauling the corpse off her, throwing it to the side.

Rosalie scrambled upright and made as if to run, but her feet were once again useless, not tangled in weeds this time but fixed to the ground like they had lead weights attached to them. The world seemed overly bright to her eyes for a moment, almost lost in white light, and then went dark.

* * *

Something was tapping on her cheek, not lightly but not quite a slap. Rosalie's eyes flew open as she remembered. She struggled to a sitting position. The person who'd been patting her face sat back on his heels.

She stared at the stranger. She hadn't seen anyone new for well over a year. Questions tumbled through her mind, and she wasn't sure which one to ask first. Then she became aware of her attacker's lifeless body a few yards away in her peripheral vision and shuddered, turning away. She wasn't ready to think about that yet. But she remembered the feeling of miraculous relief as the nightmare pinning her down was lifted off. "Thank you," she managed to say. "You saved my life."

The man gave a short nod. He rose and walked to his horse a few yards away and came back with a canteen. "Here." Rosalie accepted it and sipped metallic water while she regarded her rescuer.

He was more of a boy than a man, slight of build, with large dark eyes and unlined skin. Despite having dark hair, which curled slightly at the ends as it reached nearly to his shoulders, his face was smooth—not even a mustache and no sign of stubble. He almost looked a bit like a girl, Rosalie thought, and was discomfited at the slight thrill that went through her at that. He sat down cross-legged next to her with an unconscious grace and leaned back on his hands a little.

"What brings you to our little valley?" Rosalie asked, surprising herself with how ordinary that sounded after what had just happened. "We don't see many visitors these days." Even leaving aside the past few months of more concerted efforts to cut the community off from the world, she'd rarely seen outsiders in her lifetime, unless it was new families moving in that had a connection to someone in the town. And she'd never left the village; no one was permitted to, save for a select few men who ventured out when needed, returning with wagons full of provisions to be distributed at the elders' discretion.

"Just passin' through, miss." The boy's voice was soft and pleasant, and remarkably calm considering he'd just killed a man.

Not just any man. Her thoughts—and her eyes—returned with a jolt to the dead body. "How did you do that?" Rosalie asked, wonder and horror and something else at war in her. "How'd you kill a chosen one?" She looked back at the stranger, whose face didn't seem to register the significance of what she'd just said.

"That what you call 'em?" he said, with an edge of grim amusement.

"Why, yes." She sounded uncertain even to her own ears. "I know him. He's—that was Ezekiel."

She saw the stranger's expression change a little, though she still couldn't read what he was thinking. "Was he your beau?"

"No!" she said hastily, her face warming. It was more complicated than that, anyway. She shivered a little, thinking of the day when her slight fondness for Zeke had died, months before he'd been chosen. She could picture the very moment, in fact: Walking her home from an evening service, he'd led her off the path and behind a cluster of pines. His arm had tightened around her waist and his expression changed, as if his handsome, smiling face was a mask that had slipped askew, revealing something cold and menacing that had been right there behind it all along. She'd only escaped when they heard a sound like someone was coming. At home, she'd leaned against the front door as if trying to hold it closed, eyes shut, trying not to imagine the other way things might've turned out.

Rosalie shook her head, banishing the memory. It was too much to explain, and not something she wanted to bring up while alone with a strange man. Just because she didn't sense any threat from this one didn't mean it wasn't there, as that night with Zeke had shown her. "He was the son of our closest neighbors. He was tested, and he was reborn, so he's one of the chosen." The words felt empty and meaningless, especially in light of how Zeke had looked when he attacked her, and how he was now—most assuredly dead.

However disingenuous her words seemed to her, she felt like she had the young man's full attention for the first time since she'd come to. "What d'you mean he was tested?" he asked, looking closely at her.

She bit her lip, regretting her words. She knew she wasn't to talk to outsiders about their practices; she just hadn't seen anyone *from* the outside world in so long that she was unused to keeping secrets. But her growing doubt had escalated exponentially at the sight of Ezekiel, one of the supposed resurrected, being killed. And at the fact that he'd *attacked* her—he seemed more like a monster than one of God's earthly representatives. She thought, not for the first time, that perhaps her community's secrets weren't sacred, but rather abominations that the outside world wouldn't abide if they were revealed.

But she wasn't about to give away any *more* information—not until this stranger gave up some of his own. She returned to her unanswered question. "How'd you kill him?"

The young man gazed at her with those luminous eyes, causing a little flutter in her stomach that was unexpected—and entirely inappropriate given the grim circumstances. Finally he smiled a little. "Reckon we each know somethin' the other wants to find out," he said. "I'll tell you a little of what I know and then you tell me about this *testing* business." He tilted his head a little. "We got ourselves a bargain?"

Rosalie found herself smiling back at him despite her attempts to keep a stern face. "I suppose so."

He sat up straighter, brushed his hands off against his trousers, and held out his right one. "Name's Kit, miss," he said. "How about you?"

"Rosalie," she said. She took his hand and shook it briefly, marveling at the slender fingers only a little longer than hers, calloused from handling his horse's reins but otherwise rather soft. She pulled her hand back, not wanting to seem to linger.

"Well, Rosalie," Kit said, "I don't know too much, but I'd say this fella you call *chosen* is more of a tormented soul. I wager he was murdered by another just like him and come back to life." He appeared to be choosing his words carefully. "It's happenin' everywhere."

Rosalie felt chilled to the bone. If Kit was telling the truth, it confirmed her worst suspicion that this wasn't a holy thing happening to her community—and it meant that escape (which she'd contemplated more than once) wouldn't free her from the horror.

"Only way they can be stopped, far as I know, is like *that*," Kit continued, nodding toward the body. His knife was no longer there—he must've dislodged it and put it away before reviving her—but the ghastly wound he'd created with it, splitting the forehead and the front top of the skull asunder, was more than enough to illustrate what he meant.

Rosalie must have spent more time silently absorbing all this new information than she realized. "Now can you tell me what *you* know, miss?" he prompted her gently.

She meant to dole out only the minimum amount of information needed to satisfy Kit—

she really did. But once she started talking, there was no stopping herself. All the horror, doubt, anger, and sadness she'd been bottling up—afraid to appear faithless in the eyes of her family, neighbors, and village elders—came pouring out to this stranger. Part of her quailed realizing she was breaking her community's wall of secrecy, but the words kept coming.

Kit listened in silence, his gaze so direct and piercing that she avoided his eyes most of the time, staring at her hands twisting together in her lap.

She didn't know how it had started, but now that she knew what the problem was, she wondered if the sickness had come with the last supply run. The wagons had returned in the night, which was unusual—they'd ordinarily travel by day and reach home in the afternoon. But other than that, nothing had felt wrong or different, not for a few more days. Maybe she was too distracted in those days— she was in the midst of her brief dalliance with Zeke, which had been exciting at first. He didn't make her feel the way she'd imagined a first love would, but he was good-looking and fairly charming, and his family had good standing in the community, so she was flattered at his attention.

So perhaps there had been signs of trouble that she'd been oblivious to. She hadn't noticed when Reverend Cleaver stopped appearing in public—by the time she realized it, she couldn't remember the last time she'd seen him. Until he reappeared, but not like before. And soon after, the trials began.

Describing them to someone from outside the community brought home the wrongness of it all and made her feel fresh horror about it—the suffocating fear each time one of her community was selected, and the gruesome ritual that followed. The chosen were never seen again—escorted to an off-limits area in the foothills that the elders claimed contained a doorway to a heavenly plane—and those that didn't rise after the test were buried under a shadow of disgrace.

The fact that none of her family had yet been tested was a relief, but there was a feeling of inevitability; one of them would be, sooner or later. And as lucky as she felt each time they were passed over during the selection process, she also felt a shift in the way her neighbors regarded her family. Families with someone who'd been tested and found unworthy were broken, going about their lives with a heavy air of loss and shame. But those whose loved ones had arisen had an air of superiority, as if they felt they too were destined for heaven. Families like Rosalie's seemed to be gradually losing standing among their neighbors, having not even been worthy of being tested, regardless of the result.

But she dreaded the eventuality. Every time another test was announced, she felt more and more certain it would be her—or her brother or sister or one of her parents—that'd be chosen. And trying to imagine watching the ceremony, which had never felt either holy or natural, with one of her family members as the subject—or facing the test herself—got more and more horrific every time she witnessed another member of the community go through it. Especially now that she felt certain the elders' intentions were misguided at best, if not malicious.

She stole a glance at Kit as she finished talking. The boy did a remarkable job of concealing emotions, but she thought he looked a little shaken.

"Well, let's go then," he said simply.

"What do you mean?" For a second, she thought he meant to help her escape, and even knowing now that the danger wasn't confined to her village, it was tempting. She couldn't leave her family in peril, of course. But she allowed herself to imagine it anyway. Riding away on the back of Kit's horse, arms wrapped around his waist for balance …

"Let's go back to town so we don't miss the ceremony," Kit said, breaking into her reverie. Rosalie blushed hard, even though he couldn't possibly know what she'd been thinking.

"You can't," she breathed, shaking her head. "I don't know what they'd do to an intruder."

Kit half smiled. "I ain't an intruder, I'm a visitor."

Rosalie's heart pounded with fear for the young man, though at the same time she didn't want him to leave. She didn't want to never see him again, and she didn't want to be the only one in the village who knew that something wasn't right.

"I'm afraid for you," she said at last. Not warning him how dangerous this seemed was out of the question.

"I'm afraid for you too, Miss Rosalie," he said. He touched her hand and she let him stroke her palm with his thumb, losing herself in his eyes. "I'll feel better if I come with you."

Now her heart beat harder for a different reason, though she tried not to show it. She couldn't think of anything to say to dissuade him, so she gathered her goats and her composure. Kit dragged Zeke's body to the thicket he'd emerged from, concealing it well enough that someone would have to be looking closely to notice it. No explanation was necessary; Rosalie understood that if the elders knew *she* knew the "chosen" weren't immortal, she'd be in more danger than everyone in her village already was. And even though he'd done it to save her life, Kit would be in even greater peril if they knew he'd killed one of the supposedly blessed members of their congregation.

She herded the goats down the slope and Kit walked nearby, leading his horse. The clouds had partly dispersed, and it was intermittently sunny now, edging toward what promised to be a beautiful sunset.

"Rosalie!" She resisted making a face at the singsong voice as a girl skipped toward her and Kit. "My goodness, who is *this*?"

Rosalie forced a smile. "Hello, Dinah," she said as pleasantly as she could manage. "This here's Kit—" she looked at him, mortified that she was on a first-name basis with him and hadn't even learned his last name.

"Jones, miss," Kit said to Dinah in his soft way, looking a little shy and even more appealing. "How d'you do?"

Relieved that he'd saved her from embarrassment, Rosalie continued. "Mr. Jones was traveling the wagon road and got a little lost, so he asked if he could stay the night before he goes on his way." She felt a pang of possessiveness as Dinah looked him up and down with frank interest.

"I surely hope they let you," Dinah said, falling into step with them. The word "they" reawakened the dread in the pit of Rosalie's stomach. "If they do, I could ask my pa if you could stay with us—we've got an extra bed." A shadow passed over her face, but she soon brightened. Rosalie could practically imagine the inner monologue as Dinah convinced herself that what happened to Zeke was an honor, that her brother was in a much better place and she should be happy for him.

"That's mighty kind," Kit murmured. "I ain't sure I'm gonna stay, but—"

"I'll go ahead and ask just in case." Rosalie's pity for Dinah over Zeke's loss—he may not have been the upstanding citizen everyone seemed to think he was, but he was still her brother—was overtaken by irritation. Really the only reason Dinah had let her be courted by Zeke in peace is because he wasn't a prospect for her, being related. Any time there was a hint of Rosalie catching the eye of a boy—and the pickings were slim in their tiny village—Dinah was always there to spoil the moment and draw attention away from Rosalie. The uncanny way she'd appeared right now, it was as if she were a soothsayer whose only power was knowing when Rosalie was even slightly interested in someone.

The blasphemous but amusing thought served to distract Rosalie from her fear, but it returned even stronger as they approached the village square. There were only two main buildings around it, standing opposite one another. One was the town hall, a structure large enough to fit everyone in the village when it was too cold to hold all-town gatherings outdoors. The sheriff, who had nominal authority at best, could be found there most days.

The other building that bordered the square was the church. Though it was only slightly more ornate than the hall, it was at least as big, and distinguished by the belfry and cross on the peak of its roof. Behind it, a sprawling compound of buildings included the church elders' residences as well as storage houses where food and supplies were kept to be doled out to residents.

Rosalie edged closer to Kit as they walked. "There's still time to change your mind and leave," she murmured, low enough so hopefully Dinah couldn't hear. "I don't know why the elders are doing this, but I don't trust them anymore." Her stomach churned as she gave voice to what would've been unthinkable a few months ago.

"Quit your worryin', miss," Kit whispered back almost playfully. She glanced at his face and marveled at how calm and composed he seemed.

As they crossed the square toward the church, Brother Osgood stepped out of the front door. Rosalie relaxed somewhat. Of all the elders, he had the gentlest nature, and she sensed that he was the least fanatical about their new ritual. The creases on his careworn face seemed to have deepened these past months, giving him the appearance of constantly wearing a concerned but kindly frown.

"Afternoon, girls," he said to the two people he recognized, while keeping his eyes glued to the one he didn't.

"Good afternoon, Brother," the girls chimed in unison.

"This is Mr. Kit Jones," Dinah said importantly, compounding Rosalie's annoyance. "He's passing through and hoping to rest here for the night."

"Welcome, Mr. Jones," Brother Osgood said evenly. If he was surprised to see a stranger, he didn't let it show. "I'm sure we can find a place for you to stay. If you come with me, I'll introduce you to the other elders, and we'll see about getting you some dinner, too."

"Mighty obliged, sir," Kit said.

Brother Osgood turned his attention to Dinah and Rosalie. "Girls, you'd better run along—your folks will be wondering where you are."

Rosalie bristled inwardly, but she was used to being treated like a child by older people in the village. Probably wouldn't change until she was married and under a husband's control, she thought glumly, not relishing the prospect.

But she merely said "Yes sir" (in near unison with Dinah again), cast a wistful and worried glance at Kit, and reluctantly headed toward home.

"Thanks for showin' me the way, Miss Rosalie," Kit called after her. Hearing his voice say her name sent a tingle down her spine. She looked back quickly and they shared a smile, and she sensed that Dinah was the annoyed one now, which gave her a moment of mean pleasure.

* * *

Rosalie's usual dread at the ceremony to come that night was tempered with anticipation of seeing Kit again—if the elders had let him stay.

She tried to imagine what he was doing as she washed up and put on a fresh frock, her blue dress with a pattern of tiny white flowers that she tried to wear as little as possible so it wouldn't fade or wear out. She combed her hair smooth and shiny and parted it in the middle, pinning it up in a coil in back. Whether she was going to see Kit again or meet her doom, she thought brashly, she could look becoming for it.

Her sister Elizabeth raised her eyebrows at her appearance when she sat down for dinner, but her brother and parents didn't seem to notice. Everyone was distracted and on edge.

They finished eating and stepped out into the darkness, walking the pebbled road together toward the village square. They didn't need a lantern; they knew their small community by heart, and the moon was large and full that night. Rosalie's heart beat faster as they drew near.

Nearly everyone had gathered by the time they reached the commons. Their number had decreased over the past couple months, but they still filled the square.

The flat grassy area, kept tidy by regular grazing of livestock and shaded by a couple of large trees, was lined with torches and lanterns attached to poles, and a number of citizens had brought their own illumination as well. People milled around, chatting in hushed voices that carried an edge of tension underneath the mundane conversations about work and weather. Rosalie wasn't the only one who found herself looking past the commons to the darkness where, in the foothills of Mount Payne, the supposed heavenly portal awaited more chosen ones.

The church bell tolled and voices quieted to a murmur as everyone turned to face the building. One by one, the elders emerged in their somber black suits. Rosalie craned her neck, exhaling with relief to see Kit next to Brother Osgood. The elder said something and gestured to the gathering and the young man nodded, walking down the steps and into the crowd. Rosalie drifted forward, feeling shy all of a sudden.

Kit's wandering gaze fell on her, and he broke into a grin and headed straight toward her. She felt herself blushing furiously and was glad it might look like just an effect of the warm orange torchlight.

"Evening, Miss Rosalie," he said. She nodded, trying to seem polite but unconcerned, and held her hand out. He clasped it gently in both of his, showing no intention of letting go, his eyes shining. She pulled away when it began to feel like others were noticing.

"You look right pretty tonight," Kit said, then looked unsure of himself. "I hope that wasn't too forward."

It probably was, but Rosalie didn't care, and her smile let Kit know that. He brightened again.

A hymn began with the elders, whose wives and children and grandchildren had gathered around them. It spread through the crowd, getting louder as more joined in. The elders walked through the clusters of people, handing out tokens that consisted of a small loop of white ribbon with a pin through it. Each person took one and pinned it to their chest on the left-hand side.

Brother Sampson threaded his way through the gathering at the side of the square where Rosalie and Kit stood. He handed out a few more ribbons, his lips moving, his baritone voice soft and mellifluous. When he reached them, Rosalie's voice caught a little, but the ribbon he handed her was white and she relaxed, picking up the melody again. Then she saw what was in Brother Sampson's hand. Her singing faltered and came to a stop.

Kit, gamely attempting to hum along to the hymn he clearly didn't know, took the red ribbon that Brother Sampson offered and pinned it on his chest with a smile. The elder gave no indication that anything was out of the ordinary and continued through the crowd, doling out white ribbons.

When everyone had one—even the elders sported them on their lapels—the hymn came to an end and another started. Rosalie could see the crowd surreptitiously looking around at their neighbors' ribbons, as they always did, and those close enough to Kit to see the red one nudged and whispered to the person next to them, and thus it spread through the entire gathering, the singing masking the soft murmurs.

Rosalie's voice had deserted her. She stared at the red ribbon. Kit seemed not to notice, still smiling as he hummed tentatively. She hadn't told him exactly how someone was selected for testing, she realized now. She wasn't even sure he'd noticed he'd been handed a different color ribbon than everyone else.

The second song ended, and there was a brief hush. Brother Sampson raised his arms. "Go in peace, my friends," he said, his voice carrying effortlessly across the quiet square.

The crowd began to talk again, but in hushed tones. They filed slowly past the church, unpinning the ribbons and dropping them into a basket held by Brother Osgood's wife.

"Kit," Rosalie breathed. He turned to her, but as she tried to find her next words, her parents joined her. Behind Kit, she saw Brother Sampson approaching.

"It's time we got ourselves to bed, Rosie," her mother said. Her eyes flicked to Kit for a moment and then away.

Rosalie bit her lip. She tried to communicate the peril he was in with her eyes as she whispered goodnight and forced herself to follow her family. She couldn't bear to look back this time, even when she heard Kit say her name, but she felt his eyes on her back. And somewhere in the darkness behind him, the portal where so many of her neighbors had been taken seemed to exert a subtle pull, drawing Rosalie and her entire community toward it like a whirlpool.

* * *

She thought Elizabeth would never fall asleep, but finally her breathing slowed, and Rosalie felt her sister's body relax next to her in the bed. She lay a while longer to let Elizabeth fall deeper into slumber—and to gather her own courage to do what she'd been contemplating ever since her doubts had begun to stir. Now, with Kit in danger, she couldn't hesitate any longer.

Rosalie edged out of the bed, stopping every few inches to make sure her sister didn't stir. She pulled on a pair of her brother's threadbare, outgrown trousers that she'd rescued from the rag bin and crept through the front room and out the door.

The village was dark and silent. She carried a lantern but didn't light it for fear of being spotted by her neighbors. She walked toward and through the now empty square, stepping quietly as she stole glances toward the elders' compound to her left. Soon after she traversed the commons, the houses ended and the ground began to slope up toward Mount Payne.

She'd studied the route of the processions carrying away the chosen ones enough times to have an idea which way to go. On a plateau a few dozen feet up, she followed a shallow groove in the rocky surface. Pushing through some brush, she came to a sheer face interrupted by a dark, gaping maw.

She paused to light her lantern, then stepped hesitantly into the opening. Everyone else in the village was convinced that one who hadn't been tested would be burned by holy fires if they tried to enter the portal. Though she no longer believed anything the elders had told them about the ritual, she half expected something to stop her—a bolt of lightning, an otherworldly guardian with a fiery sword—but nothing happened. Whatever the supposed portal really was, it didn't seem to be protected by a heavenly presence as the elders had warned.

She could see about twenty feet in front of her, and then the cave appeared to end. But as she moved toward the back wall, another opening came into view on the right. From the impenetrable darkness, a soft scraping sound came, like metal on stone.

Rosalie took a shaky breath and moved toward it.

She detected some movement in the flickering light but couldn't tell what it was. The scraping was joined by another sound, a ragged breathing, almost like a quiet snarl. Rosalie shuddered but inched forward and raised her lantern over her head.

The light spread farther and she could finally see the figure against the wall. Heavy metal loops had been embedded in the rock, holding chains—which on the other end were attached with manacles to a man's wrists and ankles.

He looked at Rosalie with marbled eyes she knew all too well. Suddenly he lunged, stopping only when he reached the short length of the chains, which snapped him back away from her again. Undeterred, he burst forward again and again, straining against his restraints.

She shrank against the far wall and scooted past Reverend Cleaver, or the shell that used to contain his soul, trying not to look at his scowling, distorted face.

Past the chained figure, the cave sloped downward, and she moved forward with care, testing each step before she put her weight down. Her chest felt tight and she couldn't help but fear what would happen if she twisted an ankle and couldn't get back out.

Water dripped from the ceiling, and some of it leaked through the top of her lantern, causing it to sputter. Rosalie shivered and put her hand over it to prevent it happening again.

Over the sound of the water, she heard something that seemed at first like rushing air from a distant opening, though she couldn't feel any breeze or movement at all.

As she got closer, she started to pick out individual noises, and her heart pounded harder in her chest.

She braced herself to run in the other direction, but she saw nothing approaching her.

And then she realized why.

The floor of the cave dropped precipitously about ten feet ahead of her. The lower section was filled with figures—maybe two dozen—

and the tops of their heads were all she could see, moving restlessly, bumping into the walls of the pit and one another.

That hectic movement held her horrified fascination for several minutes. She tore her eyes away at last and spotted a darkened opening to her right. Rosalie squinted, frowning, and edged closer. The teeming crowd below her shifted, whether hearing her quiet steps, following the light as she raised it and held it forward, or detecting her by scent, she wasn't sure. She was more engrossed in trying to work out what the alcove contained.

Light from her lantern penetrated it, and she stopped in her tracks as her mind rebelled, refusing to accept what she was seeing. But there was no escaping it. A confusion of human limbs and torsos, piled like firewood in an untidy heap. Beside the gory collection, an ax, cleaver, and other instruments lay on a blood-stained piece of cloth.

She glimpsed a face staring sightlessly from the mass of remains, still attached to a torso, and recognized it as Mary Peters, one of the last people to face the trial and not arise.

Rosalie found herself backing away and realized she was edging closer to the sea of people in the sunken area, who responded to her like flecks of metal to a magnet, drawing in tighter to the closest spot they could get to where she was standing. A couple of the ones in front raised their heads, growling and seeming to sense the air with gruesome nodding motions. She knew their faces. They'd been resurrected and brought here, supposedly through this holy portal that only the chosen could traverse.

She skittered back from the edge, her hand clutched to her chest. Even though they wouldn't be able to reach her, they felt dangerously close.

Her lantern gave a warning flicker. The wick was getting low. She started back the way she came, up the dark narrow tunnel, past her village's spiritual leader snarling and straining against his manacles to get at her, and out into the cool night air, which she sucked into her lungs in gasps as she leaned against the outside of the cave for support, willing herself not to faint.

* * *

She didn't know exactly where Kit had been taken, but she had an idea. Now that she knew Reverend Cleaver was being held in the cave, she was sure his home stood empty, his wife long dead, his children grown and in homes of their own within the same group of buildings behind the church.

Rosalie was even more positive when she saw someone sitting outside the door. Of course. A guard was always sent to the home where the chosen one spent their last night before their trial. No one called them guards, but it was painfully obvious to Rosalie, especially now, that they wanted to make sure the selected person didn't try to escape their ordeal.

The young man appeared to have dozed off at his post, judging from the angle of his head and arms. She moved forward as carefully as she could. Peering in the windows on the right side as she crept along, she saw an empty living room, an empty bedroom ... and then another bedroom with someone lying in the bed.

The window was open a crack. Holding her breath, Rosalie worked it open the rest of the way. The sill was about chest height and the opening was none too large—in her skirt and petticoat it would've been nearly impossible to fit through, let alone hoist herself up to. But in britches she thought she could just about do it. She passed her unlit lantern through, reaching to place it carefully on a small table to the right of the opening. Then she braced her arms on the sill and got the first half of her body through. As she wriggled in farther, grabbing at the edge of the table, she lost her balance and tumbled to the floor with a loud thump.

Kit was upright in a second. Rosalie could barely see his face in the faint moonlight trickling in, but she knew it was him. Before she'd even pulled herself into a sitting position, he was at her side, helping her up silently and closing the window.

They both heard the front door of the house open and froze for a second, but Kit quickly regained his wits. He grabbed her elbow and pulled her toward a wardrobe; the main section was empty and he helped her climb in and shut the doors. She heard the creak of bedsprings as he sat down, seconds before the sound of pounding on the bedroom door.

"Come in," Kit called in a bleary voice, as if barely awake.

Rosalie listened as the door opened and steps entered. Lantern light pierced the small crack between the wardrobe doors and she tried to draw back farther, though there was really nowhere to go. She breathed as slowly and shallowly as she could given her fear and claustrophobia, expecting the steps to approach at any moment.

"Heard something in here," the young guard said suspiciously.

"I had a nightmare and fell plumb out of bed," Kit said. "Guess I ain't used to it after sleepin' on the ground for so long."

Rosalie thought with dismay about her lantern perched on the table, wondering how well the guard knew the room's usual contents, fearing it looked out of place.

But the young man departed after a few more terse words. She saw the thread of light disappear and heard him walking through the front room and back outside, shutting the front door.

The closet door opened. Her eyes had adjusted to the dark, so she could make out Kit's face a little more clearly. She was amazed to see he was actually smiling a little. Of course he hadn't had the horrific night she'd had, and he probably didn't know what was in store for him the next day, or he really *would* be having nightmares.

He extended his hand and helped her out. She was suddenly self-conscious about her odd outfit of shabby men's trousers, nightdress, and shawl. If Kit thought anything of it, he gave no indication. They stood close together. Kit hadn't let go of her hand, and with no one there to see it she was loath to pull away, relishing the feel of his fingers, soft where they weren't calloused, holding hers gently but persistently. His index finger brushed her wrist in a slow caress that caused a warm, heavy reaction deep inside her.

"I'm glad you came to see me," he whispered. Before she could answer, his lips touched hers, sending a shockwave through her. She made a soft involuntary sound as she felt his left arm slide around her waist and pull her close. His body pressed against her felt even more slight than she expected. She felt his breath on her cheek, then his lips, lightly tracing her earlobe and the side of her neck.

She surrendered to the unfamiliar sensations for a few moments before her real reason for sneaking into his room came crashing into her consciousness again. She pulled away the hand that had still been entwined in his and pushed against his shoulders to break their embrace.

"Stop," she panted. To his credit and her slight regret, he immediately did as she said, lowering his arms to his sides, though his eyes seemed to shine with a new heat as he looked at her.

"I—I came to warn you," she said. "You're going to be tested tomorrow. And the elders have been lying about what happens to the chosen."

* * *

After lighting a lantern and turning it down to a dim glow, Kit led her to the bed—it was the only thing to sit on in the small spare bedroom—and settled next to her. Though she initially felt flustered to be in such close proximity, Rosalie was glad to be sitting as she started telling him about the cave. The horror overcame her again and she thought her legs would feel weak if she were standing.

Kit's face gave away nothing as she talked. She asked what he was thinking.

"Least it makes more sense than what they said was happenin'," he responded with a shrug.

"Ain't you scared?" Rosalie asked him incredulously.

"Sure I am," he said, but she wasn't completely convinced.

"What are you gonna do?" Her voice rose slightly and he put his finger to his lips; she flinched and looked toward the door.

"Well, I can't run," he murmured.

She thought about it. The guard was no doubt more awake now, and he was taller and more broad-shouldered than his prisoner, but surely Kit could take him by surprise, judging from how he'd taken down Zeke. "Bet you could," she said softly. *And take me with you.* She banished that thought with chagrin.

He shook his head. "I can't leave without seein' this trial for myself."

"You're so stubborn," she whispered petulantly.

"I'm curious," he countered with a sly smile. "And there's another reason I don't want to go …" Without warning, he leaned toward her and kissed her again, lingering on her lips. She felt her insides respond in a way that she'd never felt, not with Zeke nor with any other boy she'd fancied. Some had tried to kiss her, and she always demurred.

She didn't know why she couldn't push Kit away, why she found herself stroking his cheek. It was unbelievably soft, as if he'd never had any facial hair come in.

When she was little, she used to play with Lottie, another girl her age. They'd take their dolls into a stand of evergreen trees near Lottie's house, pretending a rock with a dent in the middle was their babies' cradle. After they put the dolls to bed, Lottie would put her arms around Rosalie's waist from behind, no doubt imitating something she'd seen her parents do, and nuzzle her hair until she turned around. Lottie wouldn't let go until Rosalie let herself be kissed—little childish pecks of course, nothing like what was happening now. But Kit's cheek felt almost as soft as Lottie's had, not scratchy like the face of one of her suitors when they would get bold and press her hand to their lips.

She paused for a moment, pulled back. "Kit?" she asked. "Are you—?" But what if he wasn't? The insult of being thought a woman in the midst of his lovemaking would surely anger him, or at least dampen his ardor. And she admitted to herself that she didn't want to do that, and didn't care what he really was. "Never mind."

Kit claimed her lips again and she felt his hand undoing the buttons of her nightdress. She gasped against his mouth when she felt his hand cup her breast through the thin fabric, and had to stifle a moan when his thumb brushed her nipple, sending tingles through her entire body.

Kit drew back and looked at her frankly, a little smile on his face, then gently and wordlessly encouraged her to lie back on the bed. He lightly stroked her through the cloth again, then pushed the nightdress aside, and she was helpless, forgetting all the horror of the day and her fear about what was to come the next.

Kit unfastened her trousers and she flushed, remembering she hadn't any drawers that would fit under them. Her hands fluttered down as if to stop him, but instead they gripped the bedcovers as he eased the pants down and she felt cool air on her exposed body. Shame and excitement were at war within her as he lightly touched her where she knew she was damp and hot. Anyone who knew a woman's body would know she wasn't displeased with what was happening to her. His fingers slipped softly along the tender spot that had been brought to a state of arousal she'd rarely felt before, and never around another person.

Rosalie instinctively pressed one hand against her mouth to remind herself not to make a sound other than the soft, ragged gasps that escaped her every time Kit administered another gentle stroke. She arched her back involuntarily as a wave of pleasure crashed through her, fully out of her control. Kit plunged several fingers deep within her and she felt herself pulsing against them in gradually slowing ripples of release.

She opened her eyes, which she'd closed at some point without realizing it, and was thankful for the lantern's dim glow. Kit withdrew his hand. She shakily straightened her clothes and struggled to a sitting position. The feeling of his fingers remained somehow, not soreness exactly but a sensation that part of her had been touched that had never before come in contact with another human being.

She tried to tidy her hair, but it was difficult in the dark and with her body feeling overwhelmed and uncoordinated. She settled for a quick plait down her back; her hair was long enough that it wouldn't come fully unbraided for a while, even with nothing to fasten the end. She tried not to show her embarrassment with Kit watching her. At the same time, she'd never felt more beautiful or womanly. Despite the fact that she was wearing her brother's britches. She almost laughed at that thought.

"You gotta get home before anyone finds you gone," Kit whispered.

"What are you gonna do tomorrow?" Rosalie asked, feeling even more reluctant to leave him.

"Don't worry about me, Miss Rosalie," he said. He kissed her lips, light but lingering. "Just make sure you don't get in trouble."

There was no way she could stop worrying, but nor could she think of any way she could help by staying here. That'd just get Kit in even worse trouble himself. With his help she left through the window much more quietly than she'd come in.

* * *

Despite the terror and excitement of the day — or perhaps because of it — Rosalie's brief hours of sleep were hard and deep. She woke with a jolt, certain she'd overslept, but the gray of dawn was just starting to dissipate.

The day passed agonizingly slowly. She went through the motions of her morning toilette and chores, distracted by flashbacks from the night before that were alternately grisly and rapturous. Her anxiety about what was to come grew, and at lunchtime she could barely eat, not that anyone else had much of an appetite. Her family picked at their food in silence. Even though the selected wasn't one of their own, she sensed more dread than fanatical anticipation.

She cleaned up the table and put on her good dress again, and they walked once again to the village center.

Off to the side of the square was an enclosure with fences as high as a grown man. The gathering villagers maintained a moat of space around the pen.

Glances and murmurs directed Rosalie's eyes to the church. The doors opened and two burly men appeared. Between them they held Reverend Cleaver.

The two young men's muscles strained visibly, but they managed to keep the thing between them upright and walking. A wide, stiff leather collar kept their former leader's head facing forward, but minute movements showed he was trying to turn to one side or another to bite at the men who held him.

Nevertheless, they did an admirable job of controlling him and making the walk to the enclosure look relatively civilized.

Next out of the church was Kit. He was also flanked by guards—not as brawny as Cleaver's attendants but tall and solid compared with Kit—whose means of control wasn't physical restraint but holstered guns that they kept their hands on. Kit's knife was missing from his belt.

Kit looked at least tense, if not nervous, as he walked docilely between the two men. He spotted Rosalie in the crowd and smiled a little. She tried to return it but couldn't muster even a semblance of one. Her hands were trembling. She drifted a little closer to the enclosure. Her hand trailed down to a pouch at her waist concealed by the fringe of her shawl.

More men stepped to the fence and opened gates at either end. Rosalie forced herself to watch as Kit and the reverend were made to enter the pen.

Cleaver lunged back against his gate as it was slammed shut, trying to get at the men who'd escorted him. But as the latch was secured and they stepped away, he gradually lost interest. Turning around, he sensed the air in a manner Rosalie found disturbingly familiar.

His pale clouded eyes seemed to fix on Kit, who stood by the gate at the opposite end, looking coiled and ready.

Then the reverend burst into action, scrambling across the grassy enclosure at Kit. The young man dodged lightly, moving to the middle. For a few minutes they continued a dance that could've seemed comical if Cleaver's appearance weren't so terrifying.

The crowd shifted uncomfortably and exchanged glances. None of the villagers had dared to evade the reverend during their test. They might back away instinctively, put up protective hands, but he was usually upon them within seconds.

The men guarding the gates showed consternation too. As Kit continued to easily elude Cleaver, Rosalie saw Brother Sampson murmur something into the ear of one of his men. He nodded and walked swiftly away.

Kit noticed the exchange too. His attention was diverted just long enough to allow Cleaver to reach him, and Kit stumbled and fell as a clawlike hand gripped his shoulder. He brought his legs up and gave a powerful kick that hit the reverend in the stomach and sent him flying.

A collective gasp went up from the crowd as their leader landed on his back, arms and legs bent unnaturally. He got up and lunged as if nothing had happened, and he and Kit were back to circling, pouncing, and dodging.

Just then the young man sent away by Brother Sampson returned. Rosalie's heart sank when she saw what he was holding.

Kit didn't see him; he wasn't going to take his eyes off his attacker again. As he backed toward one side of the enclosure, poised to dodge when Cleaver reached him, the young man pushed the shepherd's crook through the slats and hooked it around Kit's neck, pulling him against the fence.

The crowd gasped again, but it sounded approving instead of shocked. Kit flailed for a moment and then put both hands on the crook, straining to pull it away. Cleaver began his clumsy, jerky run at him, and this time Kit was helpless. His face contorted in pain and his breathing was labored, but he raised his hands protectively in front of him.

Rosalie could stand no more. She darted forward to the corner of the pen Kit was trapped in. "Here!" she screamed above the din of the crowd. She thrust her arm through the fence. Kit rolled his eyes toward her, unable to turn his head, and saw what she'd pulled from the pouch at her waist. He grabbed the knife, clutched it in both hands, and drove it into Reverend Cleaver's skull just as the creature reached him.

The throng fell silent for a stunned few moments as what used to be their leader crumbled to the ground. Then shouts rang out.

Kit struggled against the hook around his neck, but he was soon swarmed by angry men who grabbed his arms and legs. The crook was withdrawn and he was carried roughly out of the enclosure and brought to stand in front of Brother Sampson.

The elder's stance was composed, but his face projected cold fury. He raised his hands to quiet the villagers, and they obeyed almost immediately.

His voice rang out over the hushed crowd. "Friends and neighbors. We all witnessed this terrible crime. We need justice—now." His voice faltered a little. A theatrical flourish, Rosalie thought, but the crowd's sympathetic faces told her that everyone else had fallen for it. "Later we shall celebrate our leader's departure to sit at the side of the Lord. We'll honor everything he did for us down here." He took a deep breath and surveyed the rapt audience. His final words were delivered in an impassioned shout. "But for now, this cursed interloper will hang!"

The silence was shattered as the villagers roared with vengeful zeal. Rosalie's broken sob was lost in the din.

A thick rope was brought out, and one of the men worked on creating a noose. Rosalie could do nothing but watch Kit, who was still being held immobile by two men, with more standing at the ready if he resisted. His large dark eyes were fixed on the rope, and his implacable calm started to crumble.

When the man succeeded in flinging the rope over a tree branch and the noose tumbled down to dangle before him, swaying slightly, something seemed to break inside of Kit. He struggled mightily against the men to no avail. He gave up and addressed Sampson, panic in his voice. "Please, Mister, don't hang me. Why can't you just shoot me instead? Or slit my throat—I don't care. Just don't hang me, I'm begging you."

Rosalie thought she saw the elder's mouth curl, almost imperceptibly, in a cruel smile. "You're a murderer. Murderers must be hanged," he said curtly, and turned his back on Kit.

"No!" Rosalie didn't realize she was going to say anything until it burst out of her. Several people near her turned with surprise. Her paralysis broken, she ran toward the elders and the men holding Kit.

"You can't do this! He's *not* a murderer!" She turned back to the rest of the villagers. "It's all lies! If Reverend Cleaver was immortal, how'd he get killed by a mere man?"

"This young man clearly had help from Satan," Sampson shot back.

"No!" she cried. "It's because the reverend *wasn't* immortal. He was sick—and everyone he 'tested,' he made them sick too, without even knowing what he was doing." She spun to look at Brother Sampson. "They didn't pass to another world! You just corralled them in that cave like animals!"

The crowd was restless, murmuring confusedly to one another. Sampson looked genuinely surprised and alarmed.

"Don't believe me?" Rosalie raised her voice even more to be heard over the commotion. Seeing one of Sampson's men approach from the corner of her eye, she edged away from him. "Come see for yourselves!"

Brother Sampson regained his composure. "Young lady, if you're talking about the Holy Gateway, it's blasphemy for anyone not chosen to enter. Their bodies will burn here on earth, and their souls will burn in Hell."

Rosalie's arms were grabbed roughly and pinned behind her. She knew it was futile to struggle but she did anyway. She saw her mother at the edge of the crowd start to rush forward, but her father put his hand on her shoulder and she stopped. Her family huddled together, her mother meeting her eyes with horror, her father looking at the ground with shoulders hunched, her brother and sister frozen in place beside them.

The crowd fell eerily silent in the bright late afternoon sun as Kit was dragged toward the tree. The young man appeared almost catatonic: eyes glazed, barely resisting, feet shuffling limply. He nearly collapsed when they set him in front of the dangling rope; his captors had to grab his arms again to keep him upright.

One of them slipped the noose over his head and began to adjust it. Kit was facing away from Rosalie now and she could only stare at his thin, slumped shoulders, her vision growing blurry with collected tears.

A bell tinkled in the distance — so distant she wasn't even sure she'd really heard it at first, despite the hush that had come over the villagers. But there it was again. Then a slightly different ringing sound — this one more like the dull clanking of a cowbell.

More bells rang, and people looked around bewildered, their rapt focus on the hanging interrupted. Even the two men preparing the execution paused what they were doing. One of Brother Sampson's men, Lucas, frowned and hurried off toward the sounds.

Rosalie saw Kit's head lift, suddenly alert again. He didn't struggle against the rope around his neck or the two men guarding him, but his body seemed to coil with readiness.

A scream — a man's voice, chilling because she'd only ever heard that kind of cry during previous trials — split the air. Lucas came back into view, running clumsily, holding his left arm with his other hand.

"We've gotta—" he panted. "Get your guns—they're comin'!"

"That ain't gonna work," Kit called over the murmur of the crowd.

"He's right!" Rosalie cried. "You gotta let him go—he knows how to fight 'em! He can help us!"

"You there!" Kit shouted at the wounded man. "What attacked you? One of your chosen?"

Lucas nodded reluctantly, clutching his arm and looking behind him. "Was Jeb Myers," he said, his voice pinched. "He was just like Reverend Cleaver was. There's more comin' too."

The crowd milled around, increasingly agitated. "What should we do, Brother Sampson?" someone called. The elder raised his hands in a fruitless appeal for quiet. They could see figures approaching now, some stumbling haltingly, some moving quickly with unnatural jerky movements.

"Please!" Rosalie screamed. "Listen to me. Free that man—he's our only hope!"

One of Kit's captors spoke. "You really gonna help us?"

"I swear," Kit said. The man studied his face for a few seconds, nodded, and lifted the noose from around his neck. The other man released Kit's arms and stepped back.

With two of Sampson's men on Kit's side, and the ghastly caricatures of their neighbors bearing down on them, it didn't take long for the rest of the village to accept his help. Kit asked for a knife and darted toward the closest creature to demonstrate how to deal a killing blow. Some of the men brandished their own knives, while others escorted women and children to safety or hurried to get weapons.

As Rosalie watched, she felt a hand on her shoulder.

"Let's get you home, away from all this," her father said. His tone was calm but his face gave away his terror.

She shook his hand off coldly. "You were quite happy to give me up before, so I think I'll stay."

"The elders were only trying to keep you safe," he said lamely.

"Go on and leave me be," Rosalie said. "I'll not be treated like a little girl any more." She turned her back on her father, and when she looked back, he was heading for home with her mother and sister as fast as he could. She wasn't sure whether she felt more relieved or scornful; there were older, less sturdy men than her father who'd chosen to stay and fight.

There was too much else happening to sort out her emotions anyway. Kit's impromptu trainees were struggling, most of them unused to anything resembling combat. Unarmed, Rosalie stood by helplessly as men she'd known her whole life fought with inhuman versions of other men and women she'd also grown up around. It was almost beyond comprehension, but it made more sense than the testing rituals ever had to her.

A few of the living were bitten in the fray, and Rosalie wondered with a knot in her stomach if all of them would succumb to the sickness, even those whose injuries didn't seem severe.

An arm clamped around her neck from behind. She was dragged toward the church and around the side of it, out of sight of anyone else.

"It was you," Brother Sampson's voice grated in her ear. "You let them out and destroyed everything."

"I didn't," Rosalie protested, pulling at his arm with both hands. "I don't know how they got out."

The elder sighed as if disappointed, but his viselike grip on her neck didn't let up. "I might be able to reclaim my flock when this is over, but not with you around to spread hateful accusations and stir up trouble."

"That's why you chose Kit too, isn't it?" Rosalie gasped, as she fought to breathe.

"I didn't want an intruder sowing doubts," Sampson replied readily, "and he couldn't be allowed to leave and tell others about us. He threatened our safety."

"Safety?" Rosalie repeated with contempt. "You're the one who put us all in danger. How could you do this?"

"To keep you all from despair, of course," Sampson said without emotion. "To help you believe that the world still made sense, that your leader hadn't been senselessly taken from you and turned into a monster."

"So you fed us lies and killed us just to keep us in your power." Her voice was little more than a breathy wheeze.

Before he could respond, Rosalie heard a snarl behind them. Sampson cried out in surprise, and somthing jostled his grip on her neck enough so she could suck in a painful breath, coughing as her throat spasmed.

Sampson screamed and his hold loosened even more. She broke free and turned to see Lucas clamping his teeth on Sampson's throat. The elder's scream turned to a gurgle. He slumped and Lucas bent over him, latched on.

Another figure appeared behind both of them, and a blade impaled Lucas' head from the top. The snarling and biting stopped and he fell sideways, releasing Sampson.

Blood gurgled from Sampson's throat as he fought to breathe. As Rosalie attempted to tear her eyes away from that sickening sight to see who had killed Lucas, the knife came down again, this time into Brother Sampson's skull.

He collapsed lifeless next to Lucas. Brother Osgood pried the blade out, panting. He met Rosalie's horrified gaze.

"He'd have died or turned. There was no saving him." He wiped the knife off on the ground. "And he was a murderer. I know that now." He nodded gravely at Rosalie. "We have you to thank for uncovering the truth, young lady."

* * *

It was fortunate that Brother Osgood understood, because he helped tamp down the villagers' hopeless rage when Kit explained what was going to happen to anyone who was bitten, and what they'd need to do. The enclosure became a space (heavily guarded) for people to sit with loved ones until the end.

Rosalie hung back in the gathering shadows, watching the survivors handle the aftermath, not wanting to go home to her family but unsure how to assist. She realized she'd lost track of Kit amidst the pandemonium. Looking around wildly, she spotted him just in time, in the distance, riding his horse unhurriedly and unnoticed away from the square in the direction of the wagon trail.

She sought an unattended horse and climbed on with difficulty in her dress to follow him. The road was deserted as she nudged her mount to go faster. Everyone was either hiding in their homes or gathered in the square.

Kit looked back when he heard hoofbeats. She couldn't read his expression as she drew closer.

She caught up as the mostly concealed path reached the bigger trail, and they rode side by side without speaking for several minutes, stealing glances at one another.

Kit was the one to break the silence. "Where you goin', Miss Rosalie?"

Although her name on his lips gave her a thrill, she frowned. "I'm going with you."

"Hmm." Another long pause.

"You don't want me to?" Rosalie burst out when she couldn't bear it anymore.

"Oh, I want you all right," Kit said. Rosalie felt her face get hot; she glanced over in time to catch him looking back with a little smile. "But I reckon I got a lot of trouble ahead of me that I don't want you mixed up in."

She opted for an indignant stance to cover up being flustered. "You think I ain't cut out for it because I'm a girl?"

"I didn't say that," Kit replied quietly.

"I'm strong — and I can learn how to fight," Rosalie continued in a protesting tone.

"I know you could," he said, and he didn't sound like he was just trying to placate her.

"Then I'm coming with you," she said firmly.

Kit looked up at the sky, where the last remnants of sunset were fading fast. "I don't want you travelin' back alone in the dark," he said. "How about we make camp soon and talk this over?"

"That sounds just fine," Rosalie said. She hoped she'd be able to change his mind, though she felt a little less sure of herself as she realized she'd come after him in such haste, she hadn't brought any provisions at all. Just a stolen horse and her best dress, now covered in dust.

* * *

Kit found them a small plateau with a good view of their surroundings and no easy route for someone to sneak up on them. While Rosalie gathered firewood, he laid out some dried beef and fruit and hard crackers. They sat with their backs against a boulder, and he shared his canteen with her to wash down the dry meal.

Rosalie wolfed down the first few pieces of jerky, her appetite roaring back as she began to settle down from the day's events. Kit opened his saddle bag while he ate, pulling out a leather-wrapped bundle, from which he took a small dish. He scraped some char from a log in their fire and crushed it on the plate with a tiny spoon. As Rosalie watched, almost forgetting to eat in her fascination, he produced a small flask from his bag and poured a few drops of liquid onto the dish, mixing it with the now powdery charcoal. Then he unwrapped a small knife of some kind and stuck the blade in the fire until it blackened.

He shoved another cracker in his mouth and rolled up his long underwear and shirt sleeves on his left arm, pushing them as far up his bicep as they'd go. The skin was covered with small markings, each one seemingly different. She couldn't quite make them out in the deepening dusk; the flicker of the fire didn't help much either.

Kit picked up the knife and, without seeming to brace himself or hesitate, cut into an unmarked patch of skin. Rosalie flinched, but Kit didn't react at all. He dabbed away droplets of blood with a cloth, poured another splash of alcohol from the flask onto his right index finger, and dabbed it in the charcoal, which he rubbed into the wound. Rosalie saw another design appear on his arm; he'd cut so deftly and unflinchingly that she hadn't realized it was more than a straight line.

"What're you doing?" she asked, unable to contain her curiosity anymore.

Kit shrugged and made another little cut, repeating the process with the charcoal. "Somethin' I do," he said simply. Rosalie scowled in frustration, but something in his tone told her she wouldn't get any more information out of him about it, so she watched in silence while he made several more designs on his arm.

She lost count of how many new marks he added—maybe as many as a dozen—but after a while he packed up the supplies and turned his full attention to his supper. Rosalie followed suit, though she couldn't stop staring at the mysterious tattoos.

"Why were you so frightened about being hung but not afraid to die?" she asked.

Kit's eyes flicked up to meet hers and then quickly looked back down at his food. "It just come over me." He shrugged "I ain't never felt that scared before."

As Rosie puzzled over that, another question occurred to her. "How do you think they got out?"

Kit chewed thoughtfully. "That one that came after you the day before—it must of found a way out. Another tunnel maybe. The rest happened upon it eventually."

"Yeah," Rosalie said slowly. "Why all of 'em at once, though, when before only one got out? They can't—talk to each other, can they, people that are—sick?"

"No," Kit said after another pause. "I don't think they can talk to each other." He put his arm around her, and it was such a quick and natural motion she didn't have time to act demure. After a hesitation she leaned her head against his shoulder.

"I gotta go on alone tomorrow, Miss Rosalie." She stiffened but didn't pull away from him, so he stroked her back. "I like you, a lot. And I know you ain't weak. But I ain't cut out to be with nobody. Besides," he continued before she could object, "Brother Osgood's gonna need your help setting things right. They ain't bad people—your folks included—leastways, not all of 'em. They just been sent down the wrong path a ways."

Her bravado deserted her, and she sighed defeatedly. "I know when I'm not wanted."

"Now I already told you that ain't the case, didn't I?" Kit said. He lifted her chin gently with his free hand and kissed her lips, softly at first, then more urgently. She knew she should want to resist, but somehow she didn't care about that.

"Reckon we should get some rest," Kit said in a low voice. Rosalie could tell from his tone what he really meant, and felt a mix of trepidation and anticipation.

The plateau was solid rock, so Kit cut and laid down pine boughs and placed his bedroll atop them. It made it a little uneven but provided some cushioning.

Rosalie stood hesitantly by the makeshift bed, wondering if she should lie down in her dress, stiff and constricting compared with the nightgown she was accustomed to. Kit noticed her indecision and smiled. He left off straightening the bedding and came over to her. "You ain't got no reason to be modest around me." It was still unnerving to her that such a soft-spoken person could be so bold and direct. But she didn't stop him when he helped her off with her frock, or kissed her long and lingering after that.

Somehow she felt less exposed in her chemise here in the open than she had in the little bedroom in Reverend Cleaver's house, and much bolder. If she was going to go back home and never see Kit again, what did anything matter?

"What about you? I don't want to sleep near you in those dusty clothes," she said, surprising herself with her forwardness. He raised his eyebrows, then smiled and unbuttoned his shirt, revealing long underwear. He shucked his boots and pants and stood completely at ease in just his long-sleeve undershirt and drawers. She glimpsed a leather strip that appeared to be a necklace around his neck, but the front part was tucked out of sight under his shirt.

"Better?" he asked. She was too shy to look at him directly. He lay down and pulled a wool blanket on top of him, then held it open with a quizzical expression. "Gonna sleep standing up tonight, Miss Rosalie?"

She laughed despite her nervousness and settled down next to him on the stiff fabric covering the pine branches. Her laugh turned to a gasp as he rolled on top of her. With so little clothing between them, she could feel his lithe muscled body. Her hands seemed to move of their own volition, touching his shoulders and back. She'd never been this close to anyone. The feel of a body pressed against her was completely new.

Despite her inexperience, she was fairly sure this wasn't how a man would feel.

It was less a revelation than confirming a suspicion. What was more surprising was how it didn't stop her own body from coming alive under Kit's touch. As her own hands grew bolder and she roamed over that strong yet slender frame, she felt less certain about her realization. But whatever or whoever Kit was, Rosalie couldn't get enough. Knowing she never would just made her determined to take everything she could that night.

3: LIN

Savory aromas of rice with chicken wafted on the evening air, along with fragrant flashes of brewing tea and the occasional floral note of opium smoke, as Lin Yong left his camp.

He rode past the gaping mouth of the tunnel, from which the acrid odor of gunpowder smoke emerged faintly, momentarily obscuring the pleasant dinnertime smells, and past more groups of wooden huts and canvas tents. Some had emptied out, their shift just beginning; others, like his, were full of workers and the palpable relief of being done with a twelve-hour shift.

It had been a few weeks since the last of the snow had melted away—the end of a slow, wet spring thaw that had initially made things more difficult. Now that the ground was clear and the air crisp but not cold, crews were actually able to enjoy their off hours instead of creeping through tunnels of snow or deep puddles of slushy mud to huddle in their shacks until their next shift. To some of his more recent hires, who'd joined at the beginning of a long blizzard-ridden winter, life was almost pleasant now by comparison.

Almost. He thought of the two men he'd lost the week before. Wang Jun, a stalwart who'd been in his gang for years, and Li Ping, a new recruit, nervous and a little clumsy at times, no doubt responsible for the premature detonation of the explosives they'd been placing. Wang had been dead by the time news had reached Lin, but poor Li Ping had hung on for an unfortunate couple of hours, tended by their cook, who tried to stop the bleeding from the stumps where his arms had been but could only slow it—and give the kid enough opium that he didn't feel much pain and wasn't entirely aware of how dire his condition was before he finally died.

Lin sighed and passed his hand over his eyes as if to banish the images seared into his mind. It wasn't the first gruesome death he'd witnessed. Fresh horrors would eventually come, and these would lose their vividness over time.

He left the last camp behind and made a wide arc around the area they populated, looking for signs of campfires or travelers having passed through earlier. A few of his crew members had been out hunting the night before and were pursued by two white men. His men, also on foot, easily outran them, but he couldn't shake their disturbing descriptions of the way the men had snarled at them as they chased them, almost like they were pretending to be wild animals. Whether they were playing a prank or were a genuine menace, Lin didn't want anyone threatening his gang.

His horse picked its way down a slope that became more treacherous than he expected, loose pebbles causing its hooves to slip a few times, but they made it down in one piece. Still no signs of recent activity. Lin's stomach rumbled as he remembered the smell of the dinner that was probably ready and being ladled out in steaming heaps into bowls for his workers. Maybe he'd head back soon.

A shot rang out a few yards south, and his appetite disappeared. Fingering his revolver, he rode cautiously in the direction the sound had come from. It could be someone from one of the other gangs out hunting, but he wasn't taking chances.

Over a low rise, a figure became visible, and Lin relaxed somewhat. The man crouched over a horse lying on the ground. He wasn't a railroad worker, judging from his clothes, but at least the gunshot wasn't something worse than putting down a lame animal.

Lin came closer, keeping his hand close to his gun.

The man looked up as he approached, then stood. Lin could tell even before he dismounted that the stranger was a good deal shorter than him, by a foot or more, and slight of build.

"Howdy," the man said. He tipped his hat back, and Lin thought for a split second that he'd been mistaken about his sex—the stranger's delicate features had almost a feminine quality to them, and his voice was on the higher-pitched side. But his clothes and bearing seemed masculine. Just a momentary misperception.

"Evening," Lin said. "Havin' some trouble?"

The man nodded heavily. He looked to be about Lin's age or a few years younger, and white—though there was something about his features that made Lin question even that. "Horse took a tumble back there," he said. "Couldn't put his foot down properly after that. I walked him for a little while, but he wasn't gonna make it." He shook his head. "I ain't got no money and nothin' to trade for another one. You know of any ranches or farms nearby where I could find work, Mister—?"

"Lin," he finished for the man after a pause. "And who are you?"

"Pleased to meet you, Mr. Lin," the man replied. "Name's Kit … Johnson. You can call me Kit." There was something awkward and immature about his manners, as if he were much younger than he looked, or perhaps unused to being around people much. Either way, he didn't have any kind of threatening air about him. Lin couldn't imagine that he was one of his workers' pursuers from the night before.

"There's no farms to speak of, nor towns either," Lin told him.

"What about you, Mr. Lin?" Kit asked. "Got any work?"

Lin snorted. "You Chinese?"

The young man cocked his head, his dark eyes unreadable. "Don't rightly know," he said. "I never knew my parents."

"Ever done railroad work?" Lin asked. The thought of bringing a Westerner onto his crew —despite Kit's coy answer, Lin was certain he wasn't even part Chinese—seemed ludicrous, but he *was* short a few men, of course, and not expecting replacements for a few weeks. "It pays thirty dollars a month for a Chinese crew—and no matter what *you* are, you get Chinese wages if you're in my gang. You pay in for board, so you'll get twenty dollars at best—if you don't gamble or drink it away."

"I've done a lot of different work," Kit said. "And I'm a fast learner." He shrugged. "Twenty'll get me a horse. I'll do any task you set me to, Mr. Lin, if you'll hire me on for a month."

Lin gave the young man a considering look. He was slender, almost delicate, but some of the smallest men on his crew were the toughest and most resilient. And Kit didn't have the hostile, superior air that a lot of strange white men had around him. How well he'd get on with the rest of the gang, who were understandably leery of Westerners, was another question.

"You get paid at the end of the month, less your board," he said. "If you don't make it a month, you get nothing. And if you make any kind of trouble for me, you're out."

His eyes searched for signs of Kit balking at his tone, but the kid just grinned and stuck out his hand. "Deal." Lin shook, half wondering if he was light-headed from hunger to be agreeing to this.

He walked his horse back toward camp, not trusting Kit enough to have him ride in back. "You seen anybody out here acting strange?" he asked as they walked.

Kit shook his head. "There's been no other humans around, far as I've seen, for at least a day's ride."

* * *

"Kit, hey Kit!" Long Han held up a ladle of food from the kettle and picked out something small, brownish, and vaguely round. "Try this!"

"What you got for me this time, Cooky?" Kit asked suspiciously as he approached.

"Try it first, then I tell you," Long said with a grin.

Lin watched from a few feet away, chuckling. Several others in line or sitting with their bowls smiled expectantly.

Kit looked around, shrugged, and plucked it from the cook's hand. He paused like he was hesitant—all part of the ritual—then popped it in his mouth and chewed. He nodded slowly, making pleased noises, as he savored the food, then gave a thumbs-up. "Now will ya tell me?"

"It's dry oyster!" Long said, laughing.

"Cooky," Kit said with a serious expression, "I'm gonna need a whole bowl of just this, please."

The cook didn't get the whole sentence, so another man in line repeated it in Mandarin to him. Long laughed again and returned Kit's thumbs-up gesture.

When Kit had first arrived at camp several days before, right around dinnertime, and taken a bowl of chicken, rice, and vegetables, Long had eyed him warily. Kit observed the others and managed a clumsy approximation of their use of chopsticks, but when he dug out a chicken head, he paused, taking it in one hand and turning it over to look at it. Long watched expectantly for the reaction he'd been going for, but Kit merely nibbled delicately at the head, chewing off all the flesh he could find and discarding the beak and skull.

"What do you think?" Lin had said, having witnessed Long's silent test with amusement.

"Mm," Kit said. "I ain't had meat this good in months." He held up the last bit of chicken neckbone in his hand and called over to Long. "Thank you kindly, Cooky!"

Long had looked startled but pleased, and it became a game for him to highlight the ingredients other Westerners had balked at, making Kit comment on each one—Kit in turn attempting to outdo himself on the extravagance of his compliments about every new food Long introduced him to.

If nothing else, Lin was glad he'd hired Kit for the amusement he provided Long Han. The man was the best cook he'd ever had in his time with Central Pacific, so it was especially galling when the few white men he encountered—visiting railroad executives or supervisors of other gangs, mostly—expressed disgust at his cooking. He didn't fault Long for now going out of his way to try and shock outsiders.

It seemed to break the ice with some of Lin's other men as well. Several of them had taken Kit under their wing in the past week, training him on the job as well as teaching him how to play wei chi and speak scraps of Mandarin.

Lin was actually impressed with Kit so far. He'd had serious doubts about his work ethic and wits based on the Westerners he'd observed over the years, and he wondered how committed the man would be, knowing he was only planning to stay for a month.

But Kit had thrown himself into every task he'd been asked to handle, from taking shifts as tea boy—hauling kegs of tea on a yoke throughout the work site and distributing it to the men—to learning how to drill holes in the rock face so gunpowder or nitroglycerin could be placed. He was strong and agile—and deferential to Lin as well as the senior men in the crew. That was something Lin had been especially watchful about—he couldn't afford, nor would he have tolerated, challenges to his authority or the natural order of the gang.

Still, some didn't accept Kit as readily. He politely declined to take a daily bath with the others—which wasn't that unusual for a white man but irritating and offensive to some of his men—and often disappeared at night when the rest of the men were getting ready for bed.

Lin didn't think it was so strange that Kit left at night—he himself lit out sometimes for the temporary town on the outskirts of all the camps to visit his woman Inola, who'd moved back there once the worst of the winter was over. Many men would give up a badly needed few hours of sleep—and a bit of their pay—to find occasional relief from their loneliness with one of the women in town.

But some of his workers were convinced Kit was connected somehow to the men they'd encountered while out hunting. "He's spying on us for the others," Lin heard one of his men,

Wu Yan, whisper to another during a game of wei chi. "He goes to meet them at night."

"If that's true, what are they waiting for?" the other man asked, sounding confused.

"We'll find out soon," he replied ominously.

Wu was deeply superstitious and even more skeptical and fearful of outsiders than the rest of the gang. "He carries a curse with him at all times, written in blood in a demonic language." That was another one of his accusations about Kit. "He bears marks of the demons on his skin—that's why he won't bathe with us."

Lin had yet to hear Wu explain what the curse had to do with the mysterious men Kit was supposedly going out to meet and give information about the crew. But he wasn't surprised by his paranoia. Wu had rituals and beliefs no one else had ever heard of. They weren't part of any recognizable folklore or religious practice and had mainly been concocted, as far as Lin could tell, by Wu's family back in Guangdong, an isolated, sheltered clan who lived on a remote farm.

Lin had been in the United States for nearly a decade, and as harsh as life was here, he already considered it his home. Many of his crew also planned to stay permanently once the railroad was completed—which was coming closer every day. But Wu had come to America reluctantly on the advice of an uncle and often spoke longingly of China and returning to his family once he'd earned enough money.

Lin didn't worry too much about Wu's ravings—he didn't think he'd be able to stir up much trouble when the other men already considered him eccentric. Plus, he didn't make any public accusations or cause any scenes, so Lin hadn't been given a reason to confront him about his wild beliefs. He just listened and watched for signs of trouble.

The first real rumblings of unrest came about a week and a half after Kit's arrival. A few men had ventured out past the camps to hunt game again, Kit included. The group came racing back an hour or two later, breathless and wide-eyed, with a bizarre story: One of the strange attackers they'd seen before had come at them again.

Their descriptions sounded like the stuff of legends and folktales. The man had eyes paler than his skin and gave off an odor of the grave. All the men's stories were consistent, though; they claimed Kit had knocked the man down and plunged a knife into his head, killing him.

Kit had insisted they throw the body into a crevasse, where it landed a hundred feet or so below, obscured by brush and pine boughs. The men, convinced the attacker had been supernatural, were more than happy to help remove it from sight. They claimed it felt and smelled like a long-dead corpse as they hauled it over the side.

Lin wrestled with what to do. If Kit had killed someone in self-defense, he didn't want to report it to railroad police, who were suspicious and hostile to Chinese teams as it was. Their mere association with Kit could be enough to start trouble for his gang and himself. But some details of the men's story raised more questions than they answered. Lin generally believed in certain supernatural elements in the world but had never actually encountered any proof of them. Part of him wondered if the incident was some sort of shared hallucination, or whether the men had concocted the story together to cover up a far darker occurrence.

Whatever the truth was, the event increased a division in the group. The men with Kit on the trip regarded him as a hero, while some of the other men now thought of him as a troublemaker and seemed even less willing to accept him. And Wu of course selected elements of the story to feed into his narratives about Kit being in league with mysterious men outside the camp, or with demons, or somehow both simultaneously.

Lin himself watched Kit's behavior even closer, but he was as even-keeled and eager to please as ever, seemingly unaffected by whatever had really happened. That was unnerving in its own way, but Kit didn't give

Lin any reason to find fault with his conduct as an employee.

* * *

It had been a fruitful couple of weeks despite the distractions and unrest in camp; together with the other gangs, they'd been making over a yard of progress per day on the tunnel. The fine weather made working conditions much more bearable than they'd been during the relentless winter, and the workers were in high spirits.

Lin ventured into the tunnel to inspect progress when he wasn't supervising other work along the route that would soon be laid with tracks. One day he accompanied Kit, who was performing tea duties that day, making it seem like a coincidence that they happened to be going the same way at the same time.

"How are you coming along, Kit?" he asked casually as they walked. He slowed his pace so the smaller man straining under the yoke and two full kegs could keep up with him.

"Mighty fine, I think, Mr. Lin," Kit said. "I hope you ain't had any complaints about me, sir."

"No," Lin said. Technically, none of the men who didn't like Kit had brought any of their issues directly to him, and overheard grumbles and second-hand rumors didn't qualify as complaints. "I'm very pleased with your work. Sure you don't want to stay on a little longer than a month?"

Lin slung his arm over the young man's shoulders, and Kit beamed at him. Lin thought, not for the first time, that Kit was almost pretty enough to be a girl. "I wish I could, sir; I like it here." His smile was unguarded, almost childlike, but fleeting. His eyes went distant, brows knitting together. "But there's somewhere I gotta be gettin'."

"Where?" Lin asked. He wasn't surprised when Kit shrugged and muttered something vague. The kid never gave up much information about himself.

It was probably for the best, Lin reflected. The stirrings of trouble among his workers were mild, but he'd rest easier when Kit was gone. Still, in the short time he'd known him, he'd grown to like the kid—they were probably only a couple years apart, but he'd come to feel protective of him, like an older brother.

They entered the tunnel, gradually leaving daylight behind. Two of Lin's gang passed them pushing a cart full of rocks and debris in the other direction. It didn't get completely dark, but the few lanterns strung up on the walls were welcome beacons, providing just enough illumination that they could watch their step.

As they neared the dead end, the sounds of chisels and drills made it harder to hear anyone talk. Lin could see some of the holes in the rock were nearly deep enough for the explosives. Kit moved away from him and gradually the drilling wound down as more holes were completed and workers paused for their tea.

Lin shook his head, almost laughing, as he watched Wu rebuff Kit's offer, his eyes clouded with suspicion. Lin had a few words with the men on drilling duty, then turned to make his way out before they placed the nitroglycerin.

In the relative quiet of the men's tea break, Lin heard something coming from the direction of the tunnel opening. It sounded like shouting, which wasn't that unusual in the course of a work day, but the panicked tone was. Lin's stomach lurched as he pictured another horrific injury. He broke into a jog, but he'd barely gotten ten feet before a wall of noise and smoke sent him reeling back. He stumbled and fell, his ears ringing, the frightened voices around him sounding distant.

Pulling the kerchief tied around his neck over his nose and mouth, he staggered to his feet, coughing, waving frantically at the air around him to try and see through the haze. On all sides, one by one, candles and lanterns flickered to life. The dust began to settle, but the indirect light from the mouth of the tunnel was gone, so visibility was still poor.

"What happened?" Lin shouted when he could speak, his brief words triggering another coughing fit.

"It's Chen!" someone shouted back. Lin squinted and saw two men approach, supporting a third one who sagged between them. He stumbled forward.

The man in the middle raised his head with effort, and Lin recoiled. The side of Chen Wei's face was bloody, and his eyes were unfocused. He was bleeding through his shirt in several places as well.

"He was bringing some explosive and it must've gone off," one of the other men said. He was covered in dust and debris but seemed unhurt. Looking at Chen's injuries, Lin thought he had to have dropped or thrown the nitroglycerin before it detonated; otherwise there wouldn't be much left of him.

"He attacked me," Chen said, his voice weak and choked. "One of the white demons."

The other men gasped. Lin remembered that Chen had been one of the hunters who had witnessed both alleged attacks. "Like you saw before?" he asked.

Chen nodded, his eyes growing more distant, his body shaking.

"They bit you?" Kit asked. Lin turned in surprise; he hadn't noticed him approach. Chen didn't seem to understand the question even though his English was serviceable. Lin was baffled but repeated it in Mandarin.

"Yes," Chen answered. He nodded his unsteady head toward his left shoulder. Lin pulled his shirt back. One of the bloody patches wasn't from debris—he could see that the flesh had been torn as if a wild animal had latched onto him.

"Mr. Lin," Kit said in a low but urgent voice.

Lin tore his eyes away from the ugly wound. "What?"

"He's done for, sir," Kit said. "We gotta put him down or he might turn like the one who bit him."

"Put him down ..." Lin couldn't comprehend it for a second. "You mean kill him?"

He heard one of his men whispering in Mandarin. "Kit wants to kill Chen." The wounded man himself was apparently too dazed to take that in, but several others shouted in protest.

"Quiet!" Lin roared, and the tunnel fell silent. "No one is killing anyone." He repeated that in English for Kit's benefit, firmly. "No one is killing anyone."

Kit tugged Lin's arm, and he reluctantly took a few steps away, leaning down to listen. Lin could feel the other men's eyes on his back and hear their suspicious mutters. "You gotta believe me," Kit said.

His whispered words spun an unbelievable story about dead men and women coming back to life as monstrous creatures that attacked their own, infecting their victims with a deadly poison that killed them and then turned many of them into monsters themselves.

These were the things that had chased the hunters, Kit claimed. He'd killed several in the area before joining Lin's crew—as well as the one on the hunting expedition the other night—and patrolled the area each night after dinner, occasionally catching another.

He hadn't wanted to raise the other men's suspicion of him any further, and there were so few around that he thought he could handle it himself. He'd planned to warn Lin before he left at the end of the month, because if one of them got into the densely packed camps and infected several men, it could spread like wildfire.

That's why they needed to kill Chen, Kit insisted. The explosion had blocked the tunnel and there was no telling how long they'd be trapped. Sometimes people went a little crazy even before they seemed to die and come back—he knew of a man who'd bitten and infected several people while still apparently alive himself. He explained that usual methods of killing didn't work on these creatures—they had to be dispatched by a decisive stab through their brains.

Lin was torn between disbelief and anger. If this was somehow true, then Kit had deliberately withheld life or death information. At the same time, Lin wasn't even sure he believed it now, and that was after having seen

Chen's wound. He couldn't imagine how much more skeptical he'd've been before, so he could on some level understand why Kit hadn't tried to tell him until now.

He turned to look at the upset workers milling around Chen. Several men had removed their shirts and laid them on the ground so they could make the wounded man as comfortable as possible. He was still on the verge of unconsciousness, his head moving from side to side, his breathing visibly labored.

"I'll take your word that you're telling the truth," Lin told Kit, "and I won't let anyone get hurt. But we do it my way, understand?"

Kit's pause worried him—if he didn't go along with him, Lin wasn't sure he could control the other men's reaction. Finally Kit sighed reluctantly. "Yes sir."

Lin called the men in the tunnel to gather around them. He told them an abbreviated version of Kit's story, stopping several times to silence them when their shocked and skeptical reactions became too loud for him to be heard over.

"Don't you see now?" Wu shouted at one point. "He's in league with these demons—how else can you explain their appearance just when he came to us?" Lin could tell Wu had a more receptive audience than usual for his ravings, but he managed to quell the crowd once again.

"We won't kill Chen," he said loudly and firmly. "We must stay safe, though. When we've done all we can for his injuries, we'll put him away from the rest of us, guard him to make sure he can't attack us. If he becomes a monster as Kit has warned, then we may have to stop him. But we won't act in haste." He saw Kit straining to catch what he was saying, and repeated the gist of his plan in English for his benefit. Thankfully, the young man didn't object.

The men moved Chen gently to a far end of their prison and dressed his wounds with what they could scrape together, cleansing them with strips of the least dirty clothing among them dipped in a cup of green tea. They had no opium or anything else to dull the pain, but

Chen seemed unaware of his surroundings. That was some blessing at least. And, Lin reflected, he seemed far too weak to attack anyone, so he doubted Kit's prediction would come to pass.

They inspected the tunnel cave-in. It was a new wall of rubble with no passable openings—they had no way of knowing how thick the obstruction was, but it seemed substantial. They heard, faintly, banging sounds on the other side that they hoped was a rescue party that would reach them soon, but their shouts went unanswered.

While his crew started working on the rubble pile on their end, Lin surveyed their provisions. They had little food to speak of, but the two kegs of tea Kit had carried in were still more than half full, so they wouldn't go thirsty for a while if they rationed it.

A few men, including Kit, kept a vigil over Chen Wei. Soon a shout went up from the group. "He's dying, he's dying!" Lin raced to where they stood a few feet from Chen. Despite the spreading mistrust of Kit Johnson, they'd apparently taken enough of his story to heart to keep their distance, even as their friend's body spasmed, fighting for breath.

Lin couldn't leave Chen suffering in isolation like that. He pushed past the cluster of worried workers and knelt by him. Chen's eyes were open again but staring past him like he wasn't there. He whispered too faintly for Lin to catch any actual words. Lin held his hand, helplessly watching him spiral toward death.

At last his eyes closed and his body relaxed. Lin leaned forward and listened, hoping to hear at least a faint breath, ignoring Kit's shouts to be careful. He touched Chen's heart, neck, and wrist, searching in vain for signs of life.

At last he stood and turned. "Chen is dead." There were groans and sighs. Like many of the men in Lin's gang, Chen was several years older than him and had a wife and children back in China that he'd hoped to bring to America one day. Lin had seen many such men die, but not enough to stop the stab of sorrow each time as he thought of their families.

The other men stopped their work and gathered at a safe distance, but Kit approached the body. Lin could tell from the looks on the other men's faces that they were torn between believing Kit's story and suspecting he'd brought this trouble into their midst. Lin moved toward Kit and put a hand on his shoulder. "Don't be foolish," he murmured to him. "You said some of them don't come back, so give it a chance."

Minutes ticked by feeling like hours; every eye was raptly focused on Chen's body, and no one spoke.

Then, a faint, almost undetectable sound. At first it seemed like breathing. "Chen is alive," someone whispered, and the statement passed through the crowd in a string of breathless repetitions.

Lin's eyes flicked between Chen and Kit. "Careful," Lin muttered. Kit glanced in his direction but quickly turned his attention back to Chen.

The supposedly dead man stirred. The murmurs among the men grew louder as Chen struggled to a sitting position. Lin didn't know if the other men detected it, but there was something off-kilter about his movements. Lin was reminded of theatre performers, mimicking human motion but in exaggerated, artificial ways.

Chen's eyes opened, and those close enough to see them gasped. They were pale and clouded, seemingly unseeing, though he turned his head from side to side as if surveying his surroundings—or scenting the air like a predatory animal.

Then he was on his feet, unsteady and clumsy, but not because he looked to be in any pain. His lips peeled back from his teeth, and he began to growl in a strange, voiceless way.

Kit sprang into action, drawing his knife and stalking toward what used to be Chen with an alert grace that was in direct contrast to the artless, unnatural movements of the creature.

Before Lin could react, Wu and two other men shoved past him. They clutched Kit's arms and tried to yank him backward, away from Chen.

The latter chose that moment to launch himself at Kit, who struggled mightily against the men restraining him but was unable to even lift his knife. He managed to get his left arm partway up in front of him, still held by the other men, and Lin watched aghast as Chen—a gentle, generous man who'd always been kind to Kit and whom Lin had never seen so much as raise his voice to anyone—opened his twisted mouth and clamped his teeth down on Kit's upper arm.

Kit screamed, a high-pitched sound that pierced the air, and tried to pull away, but Chen stayed affixed, his growls muffled by Kit's shirt. The three men holding the boy let go and backed away, then turned and ran past Lin, wide-eyed with terror.

Kit's left arm was still lodged in Chen's jaws, but now that he was free from the men restraining him, he transferred the knife to his right hand. Lifting his arm over the creature's head, he brought it down with all his might. Lin watched, horrified, as the knife crunched through the top rear of Chen's skull and lodged deep in his head.

Chen's body went limp again. The snarling stopped, and Lin could now hear Kit's breathing, a low whining of pain accompanying each exhalation, as he pried the clenched teeth off his arm. Then he pulled the knife out of the corpse with grunts of effort that sounded almost like sobs.

He wiped the blade carelessly on his trousers and resheathed it, then paused over the corpse. Lin and the other men maintained a wide berth around the scene, so Kit was alone with Chen. He leaned down, his wounded arm hanging by his side, and used his good one to touch the dead man's shoulder. He recoiled almost immediately, then did it again.

Kit stayed motionless for several seconds, then straightened and turned. Eyes shining with tears, he approached Lin. "I can't hear him at all," he said. He gestured at his mauled arm. "I guess it's 'cause I'm done for." He laughed bitterly and took his knife out again. Lin flinched backward a step, but Kit merely held the weapon toward him in his open palm. "I can't do it to myself—wouldn't be able to get the blade in far enough before I lost my nerve or hit the deck, most likely. You need to do it for me, sir."

Lin took the knife, shaking his head. "You ain't even hurt that bad," he said. "You might pull through if we clean out that wound."

"Don't you get it?" Kit asked, his face a mask of despair. "This bite'll kill me. Everyone who's bit dies, and a lot of 'em come back. It might take a couple hours, but I'm dyin'." He wobbled on his feet. "You best protect the rest of your men. I'm warnin' you." Kit's eyes rolled up into his head and he collapsed on the ground.

"You heard him, boss." Wu's voice behind him made Lin's heart sink. "Best to get rid of him now."

Lin spun around, exasperated. "You really think he's gonna die from that one bite?"

Wu shrugged. "I don't know about that, but I know he was already dangerous, and now's our chance." He gestured back at Chen's corpse. "He killed one of us!"

"You saw what happened—he was defending himself," Lin countered. "And protecting the rest of us too, for that matter."

"From an evil that *he* brought into our camp!" Wu said.

"I don't think so," Lin said. "He's been helping us, fighting them."

"Then he's planning something worse." Wu was undeterred. "He's in league with demons, boss. Look at that spell he carries around. Look at the marks on his arms."

"Back off, Wu," Lin said sternly. He raised his voice again, though there wasn't much din to be heard above this time—the men's murmurs were hushed and frightened. "We'll give Kit the same courtesy we did Chen," he announced. "Treat his wound as best we can, then let him alone and watch him to see if he dies and if—the other thing happens to him."

Wu protested, but no one joined him. Kit had been proven right about Chen and had shielded the rest of them from being attacked, so they were willing to give him a chance.

They moved him, by tacit agreement taking him to the opposite side of the tunnel from where Chen's body lay. Lin took on the task of treating Kit's injury; he hadn't completely dismissed the possibility that Wu or one of the other men would try to harm him.

He unbuttoned the young man's shirt and removed it from his good right arm, then slid it under his barely conscious body and pulled it gingerly off his left. The drying blood caused it to stick to the underclothes and skin underneath. Kit moaned each time the wound was touched or the arm jostled, his eyelids fluttering, but he didn't fully awaken.

When at last the shirt was off, Lin hesitated over the undershirt. He undid the single button at the neck, but pulling the shirt over Kit's head would be too rough. He picked up Kit's knife again and cut the left sleeve off at the shoulder, then slit it lengthwise. It fell away except where it was stuck in the blood around the bite. Lin tugged the fabric gradually away. It was stuck on worse than the top shirt had been, but he detached it at last.

"Look, boss," one of his men said in a hushed voice. Lin had been concentrating so intently on being gentle with the wound that he hadn't even noticed the strange marks on Kit's arm.

He brought a lantern close. There were dozens of them, marching down the arm in orderly rows. They were no letters or characters Lin had ever encountered, and he had a knack for picking up written languages, having encountered several during his time in America. It really didn't look like a language at all. Each symbol on Kit's arm was slightly different, or seemed so at first glance.

"You see now, boss?" Lin didn't have to look up to know it was Wu, and he didn't bother to answer him.

"Someone clean this wound," he said. One of his men got some tea and started dabbing at it with a bit of cloth. Lin didn't need to remove the rest of the shirt, but he was curious himself now. He cut the right sleeve off and saw more symbols, not as many and not as neatly spaced or crafted.

As he'd cut, his arm had brushed against something else under the shirt where it covered Kit's belly. He cut from the V where it was unbuttoned all the way down to Kit's waistband; the undershirt was already destroyed anyway, he thought to himself. He untucked it, cut the rest and pulled it open fully.

Everyone around him seemed to start talking at once.

A square of oilcloth wrapped around something lay on Kit's bare, slender belly. Around his neck, a thin strip of leather with some sort of charm attached to it, not fully visible because the weight of it had caused it to slide off to the side of his neck.

Neither the bundle nor the necklace were what had drawn the most attention. It was the other thing the undershirt had concealed: a wide strip of white linen, wrapped tightly around Kit's chest.

Lin sat back on his heels, the oilcloth package in his hand momentarily forgotten. There were no signs of injury on Kit's torso, and the cloth was clean—no visible bloodstains—so it didn't seem like a bandage. It almost looked like a primitive version of the dudou that women wore back home to bind and flatten their breasts.

"Turn away," he said, looking around sternly at his men's curious faces, willing them not to challenge him. All of them (even Wu) thankfully obeyed, and he loosened the knot that held the cloth in place. He unwrapped it carefully in case it concealed an injury of some kind, but Kit didn't react in pain or seem to know what was happening. Lin opened it just enough to confirm his original thought was correct, then refastened the binding as close to its original configuration as possible, his mind racing to adjust to this new reality. "Just a scrape, nearly healed," he said, as if to himself but for the benefit of the men, who turned back toward him and soon crowded around again.

"That's what I've been trying to tell you about, boss!" Wu pointed at the bundle in Lin's hand, stabbing his finger toward it emphatically. "I saw him looking at it once. See for yourself—it's got to be a curse."

Lin didn't acknowledge Wu's ranting. "Everyone back off now." He pointed at a couple of his more level-headed men. "Stand guard and let me know if it seems like Kit is about to die."

He took the cloth-wrapped object to a spot away from the others and positioned a lantern on the ground next to him as he sat down and opened it. Inside, a brittle piece of paper, folded twice to form a small rectangle. The visible side was a wanted handbill about a horse thief; it looked hastily created and didn't include a drawing, just crookedly printed words.

He unfolded it gingerly, noticing flecks falling from it as he did so. On the other side of the paper from the wanted notice was something scrawled in what first looked like paint but, on closer inspection, he reluctantly concurred with Wu's wild theory that it was blood. A good amount of the original writing in the substance had fallen away, leaving only faint stains, and it looked like some of the marks had been gone over in pencil where the blood had flaked off.

The messy, faded, chaotic combination of dried blood, faded bloodstains and pencil marks looked like gibberish at first. But then he recognized a character, and another, and realized what it was.

While staying with Inola one winter in Nevada before he joined the railroad, he'd come across newspapers from back east and letters from her father in an unfamiliar language. He asked to learn it, and she'd taught it to him to pass the time while he looked for work.

He was out of practice, but once he recalled a few more characters, it came back to him in a rush. That's how his brain worked when it came to languages. Marks became words and suddenly the page was speaking to him.

His mouth went dry and his heart ached as he read the frantic words of a dying woman to her newborn child.

* * *

The hours wore on with no rescue, no breakthrough on the cave-in, and Kit seemingly clinging to life, not quite conscious but still breathing and moving a little under Lin's shirt, which he'd removed and draped over Kit's upper body. The men rested in shifts, taking turns working and watching Kit.

Lin dozed off, propped against one of the tunnel walls, and came awake with a jerk, his shirtless body chilled, not knowing how much time had passed. Wu was next to him, and he groaned under his breath.

"Boss?"

"What is it, Wu?"

"Did you look at the demon's curse he carries, written in blood?"

"Yeah," Lin said. "It's not what it seemed to you." He took the paper, which he'd carefully refolded, from his pocket, and Wu flinched, shrinking away but watching with fascination as Lin unfolded it.

Lin winced as more brownish red flecks flaked away, but he turned it over to show Wu the side that was printed with English. He pointed to the words, translating into Mandarin. "Wanted. Dead or alive. The horse thief George Goodwin. Last seen with accomplices: sons Charles and John Goodwin and wife Maisie. Stole two horses from Fort Hodgkin near Oak Bluff, Nebraska Territory. Bring information to Bill Peterson."

Wu shrugged uncomprehendingly. "That's just the paper they used. Look at the other side."

Lin turned it slowly and Wu whispered something unintelligible under his breath. "It's Cherokee," Lin said. "It's an Indian language." He reread the lines silently and spoke the equivalent in Mandarin. "My only child. We fought to stay alive for you but were betrayed and murdered. Though we are gone, know the family that loved you. Your father George

Goodwin. Your mother Maisie. Charlie and Johnny, your half-brothers." The syllabary didn't quite capture the names but Lin knew what they were meant to be from the wanted notice. "Know where you came from. English and Scottish settlers, and the Ani-Yunwiya of Ustanali. All of us will live forever in you."

Wu had moved closer as Lin read, his expression transformed from fear and suspicion to wonderment. "It's not a curse." He shook his head. "But it's a powerful spell." He looked back to where Kit lay. "You should return it to him. He needs it now."

* * *

"Boss." Lin struck the rock once more and turned. Wu hovered behind him, looking worried. Since he'd had the document read aloud to him, he'd barely let Kit out of his sight, watching the semiconscious man closely from a few feet away. "He's awake. He's saying something."

Lin handed his sledgehammer to another man and followed Wu. Kit was stirring, eyes open, muttering something Lin couldn't make out. Wu hung back at the invisible barrier around Kit, but Lin moved closer and knelt by him.

Kit's eyes turned toward Lin. They were bright and shiny with hectic energy in a face that was flushed and moist, but at least they weren't pale or cloudy. "Help me," he said in a thin, raspy voice.

"I want to help you, Kit," Lin said. "What can I do?"

"Don't know," Kit said. "There's somethin' fightin' me. Inside."

"You ain't changed though, and you ain't dead," Lin said. "There's hope."

Kit tried to answer, but his eyes rolled back in his head and his body went limp.

Lin held a lantern close to Kit's right arm. The wound looked exactly the same—it hadn't begun to scab over but there was no sign of an infection spreading. Lin sat back on his heels. Kit twitched occasionally, moaning under his breath.

"Boss." Wu again. "You gave it back to him, right?"

"You saw me," Lin said with a hint of frustration.

Wu crouched next to him, staring at Kit. "It's not enough," he said. "He needs the blood of his family. He needs his mother's spell."

"What?" Lin looked at him with bafflement.

Wu reached toward Kit and drew the packet out from under Lin's shirt. "I can make him a medicine," he said. "The blood of family. It helps when someone is very ill." He opened the oilcloth with reverence—a stark contrast from the frightened way he'd recoiled from it before—and unfolded the paper, scraping at some of the dark brown lettering. It flaked off easily under his fingernail. "This has to be her blood," he said. "Usually the medicine is made with blood that's fresh, from someone living. But this letter is a strong charm. His mother wrote all of his ancestry into it with her very blood. It might work."

Lin frowned doubtfully. It felt wrong on so many levels, but especially to desecrate this possession of Kit's for something that sounded to him like a foolish superstition.

Wu put his hand on Lin's arm. "Please, boss," he said. "Let me try. I was wrong about Kit. Let me try to make things right."

With much misgiving, Lin assented. Using a stone, Wu ground much of the dried blood on the paper into a powder. He mixed it into a small amount of tea. "Hold his head up, boss."

Lin lifted and supported Kit's head, gently restraining it from tossing back and forth. Wu held the cup to his lips, which were moving as if he were speaking, though no sound came out. Kit coughed when the liquid first entered his mouth but then began drinking. His eyes fluttered open briefly, but he didn't appear to register the two men's faces above him. Wu tipped the cup, coaxing the last few drops into his mouth.

When Kit had swallowed most of the liquid, Lin lowered his head gently to the ground again. The wounded man slipped into what looked like a peaceful slumber, his breathing unlabored for the first time in hours, and Lin and Wu moved away from him again to continue their vigil at a safe distance. Lin didn't sense any danger, but he wasn't taking any chances.

He left to check on the progress of the men chipping away at the fallen rocks. They could hear the banging from the other side more clearly now; it seemed the barrier was growing thinner. Lin relieved an exhausted man of his hammer and took his place.

* * *

Not the bright sunlight that they'd left to enter the tunnel hours ago, but gray dull dawn greeted them through a small opening in the rubble. The shouts of the men on both sides were jubilant though. With renewed energy, they hacked and hauled away and soon there was an opening big enough for one man at a time to crawl through.

Lin dropped his sledgehammer, his chest beaded with sweat that cooled rapidly in the air coming through the opening. He watched a few of his men slither through the tight space, then walked to the rear of the chamber to check on Kit.

He looked deep in slumber, but his face had lost its flushed, feverish look and he wasn't tossing and turning. Lin shook his shoulder gently, then patted his cheek.

Kit's eyes drifted open, and Lin was relieved to see they were still their usual color, and—though dazed with sleep—more alert than they had been since the attack.

"How do you feel?" Lin asked.

Kit raised his head, then sat up. He smiled with relief. "Better." Lin's shirt that had served as his blanket had fallen from his shoulders, and they both looked at his right arm. The wound was well on its way to scabbing over. There was bruising around the teeth marks but no sign of infection or swelling. "I can't believe it," Kit said. "I never seen this happen to anyone who's been bit."

Lin sighed, dreading what he had to tell him next. "I don't know if it made any difference, but Wu made a … special remedy for you."

"Really?" Kit grinned, looking more and more like himself. "Wu did that for me? Will wonders never cease."

Ordinarily Lin would've been amused, but he had to tell Kit what it had been made of. As he did, the man's face went white, his expression stricken. Lin handed him what was left of the document, the letters virtually stripped away, though faint stains remained where the blood had been.

"I'm sorry about this," Lin said.

"It's—it was my only hope of findin' out anything about my family." Kit's voice was hollow. "I never could figure it out. Always hoped I would one day."

"You didn't know what it said?" Along with Lin's surprise came a wave of relief. He had something to offer in return for destroying the heirloom.

Shouts came from the other side of the cave-in and Lin flinched; his frayed nerves and exhausted brain were jolted back to high alert. He raced back the way he'd come and climbed the pile of debris toward the hole.

"What's going on?" he called to a man who was wriggling frantically back through the opening.

"More of them," he panted. "More demons."

Lin swore. "Get that opening a little bigger," he said. "I'll never get through it." The man obeyed at once, grabbing a hammer that had been discarded and pounding at the jagged hole to dislodge more rocks. Lin yanked at some on the other end of the opening with his bare hands.

Someone pushed past him, nearly knocking him over. He saw Kit's slender legs disappearing through the hole.

With a cracking sound, the man working with the hammer pulled a larger rock away, expanding the gap by another six inches. Lin went for it; once his broad shoulders squeezed through, the rest of his body followed more easily.

He stumbled down the other side and darted to the mouth of the tunnel. In the yellowing gray light of dawn, everything looked dreamlike as he watched Kit launch his slight frame—looking even smaller shirtless— into someone. The other person lost their footing and fell backward, and Kit was on them at once. Lin had time to wonder how Kit had found his knife on the way out of the tunnel before the blade sank deep into the skull of the man he was on top of.

As Lin approached, Kit paused over the body, his hand on the shoulder. He looked up with something like relief in his eyes. "I can hear 'em again!"

* * *

After the trail of the infected man had been traced, after everyone he'd had contact with had been checked and the wounded men isolated for observation, after a report had been made up the chain (Lin kept it brief, knowing the deaths of a few Chinese workers would be of less concern than how much of a delay the cave-in would cost the company), Lin met with Kit alone in the small office attached to his quarters.

Kit tossed back the finger of whiskey that Lin offered him. He sat in a hard wooden chair across the desk from Lin and stared at the ancient piece of paper, touching the blood stains with the tips of his fingers as Lin told him the contents of his mother's letter. His shoulders shook but his crying was silent.

Kit scrubbed his face with his sleeve when Lin finished. "Thank you," he said in a tear-clogged voice. "I ain't got the words to thank you properly, Mr. Lin." His eyes grew distant. "I knew somethin' was pulling me east. Guess I woulda got there one way or the other, but it's good to know where I'm goin'."

"Yeah." Lin had many questions, but in a way, it seemed better not to know any more than he did. He bent and unlocked a safe under his desk and emerged with a tidy stack of bills. "This should be enough to buy a horse in town. I can ride you over there today."

"But—" Kit looked astonished. "I still got over a week left in the month, ain't I?"

Lin shook his head. "What you did, and the way you've been looking out for us, saved me a lot of trouble. It would've been much worse without you. And if more come, you've shown us how to fight 'em off." He studied Kit's face. "What you're doing—where you're going—it has something to do with this, right?"

"I think so." Kit's eyes were distant as he considered the question. "I don't rightly understand it myself, sir."

Lin nodded. "Well, if there's any chance you can stop this from spreading, better to have you working on that instead of the railroad." He didn't say, though he thought it, that if there was any chance Kit was somehow partly responsible for this disease, that was another reason it was better he left.

"If you're sure, Mr. Lin," Kit said. "I'm mighty obliged." He stood. "I'll go pack my things and meet you back here?"

"Take your time," Lin said, thinking about washing up and putting on clean clothes before they headed out. He hoped Inola would be happy to receive a surprise visit from him. He couldn't wait to tell her how the Cherokee she'd taught him had come in handy. And he wanted to make sure she knew how to defend herself in case the sickness reached town.

"Thank you sir." Kit's face clouded over. "I got a few folks I'd like to say goodbye to." Lin walked him to the door of his office and watched him leave with a pang of pity and sadness that almost overshadowed his relief.

4: KIT

Alone again.

Just the way I like it, I tell myself whenever I start to feel like it's too quiet. No one to worry about, no one's safety to feel responsible for.

Once I leave Utah, Wyoming Territory opens out flat in front of me, plains covered with short prairie grass. It's almost hot during the day and cool at night. Not much water to speak of, so when I encounter a creek I follow it southeast a ways, until something inside tells me I shouldn't anymore. Then I cross it and keep going east. I cross at a point that's shallow and not too rapid; even a child could make it across on their own without too much difficulty.

I wonder, often, if this was the route I traveled when *I* was a child, when I was carried west to California. I didn't find out I'd been adopted until I was about to leave home forever, so I don't know the exact story of how I came to be with the folks who raised me as their own. But still I wonder if this landscape passed by my eyes before, if I carry similar images somewhere in my memory.

None come to me—it looks unfamiliar—but something tugs me along, shows me where to go. Like a compass needle I can feel but not see, that starts to wobble if I go too far off course.

The memories I do have crowd my mind. Mostly of suffering and horrors, but some others that make me smile like a fool at the scrubby empty land in front of me.

Late one morning a fat, slow-moving rabbit bounds in front of me. My horse rears up, almost throwing me off, but I hang on and squeeze off a shot that gets lucky, going straight through the rabbit's brain. I've started wearing a pistol I took off one of the infected sometime between leaving Rosalie and getting to Mr. Lin's camp. I haven't had much cause to use it except when I shot my horse back then. But I'm running through my food supplies faster these days so I keep the gun handy, and it's paid off.

It's a cloudy day, not unbearably hot even though it's about high noon, so I build a fire right there, and skin and spit my kill. It's a juicy, satisfying lunch. I'm surprised a rabbit managed to live such a life of plenty in this rugged place.

There's plenty left over even after I'm stuffed. "I can't eat another bite," I say to myself, loudly. I leave it impaled on a stick, propped up by the smoking cinders of the fire, and ride away slowly.

I don't look back, but I don't go too fast for a while.

I run across a pack of the sick in the evening and spend some time clearing them out. Five of them: a gray-haired woman, a man, and three skinny stunted boys who might've been in their teens. I lay my hand on them one at a time. The man had once worn a uniform and done things to Cheyenne women and children that my mind recoils from as soon as the knowledge of it starts flooding in. I pull back fast to cut the images off.

It makes touching the woman seem tame by comparison, even though she'd tortured her three boys, starved and dominated them their whole lives. But it didn't come from nowhere; there were other things, farther back in her life, that had been done to her. So many times I encounter that; the worst monsters among the infected have usually suffered as bad as their victims at some point. Unbroken chains of evil that stretch back who knows how many generations.

The kids hadn't done anything wrong, nothing serious, in their short lives. Just suffered and tried to survive, somehow unable to leave their mother no matter how bad it got.

I get a brief glimpse of each one's past, one at a time, and it's like shards of a mirror reflecting bits of what I got from the woman.

I make a search of the area in widening circles until I find the abandoned wagon they must've been traveling in, surrounded by big patches of blood (and worse) on the ground, a half mile northwest or so. The dead come from all directions now. It used to be only from the east.

There's no others in the area, so I get back on track and make a little more progress before sunset. I take out my tools and make five more marks on my right arm. My left hand is getting more skilled at it. I heat up some beans and eat about half, leaving the pot and my canteen out. I yawn and stretch exaggeratedly, get into my bedroll, and start making snoring sounds. I crack my eye open a little to make sure any rustling sounds aren't sick ones. The next morning all the food and some of the water is gone.

The rest of the day is uneventful, just a long stretch of riding not very fast across an unchanging plain. If I closed my eyes for an hour and opened them, it'd seem like I hadn't gone anywhere at all. Only my invisible compass—or rather, its lack of bothering me—tells me I'm making progress. No sick ones appear, so there's nothing to do but let my mind wander. Soon Rosalie's in all my senses, her scent and her hungry lips and her bold, curious hands, her hair tumbling around us as I pull her on top of me.

I lose track of how much time passes as I relive those times over and over. But as always happens, I'm left with the image of her tense shoulders, her head held high as she rides away from me.

I let myself picture catching up to her, asking her to come after all. I go ahead and torment myself with that notion for a while. But then I remember my friends at the railroad camp, their guarded faces as they say goodbye to me. Their relief that I'd be gone soon. I know it was best to send Rosalie back to her village. I know I'm not right. It doesn't take long for things around me to go wrong.

My mother—the only one I knew anyway—held out the longest. But she had the same look as Mr. Lin, that relief, when I left home at fifteen. She tried to believe I was right, but she knew better than anyone that I wasn't.

Thinking about my mother makes me glad I told Rosalie to go. The thought of ever seeing that look on *her* face is unbearable. Maybe this way, she dreams about me the way I do about her.

And I'm alone again, just the way I like it. I look back and see a moving speck in the distance. I realize I've been coaxing my horse little by little to go faster. I slow, then stop, get down and let him graze for a few minutes while I stretch my legs and watch the speck from the corner of my eye gradually getting larger.

It's been this way for a couple weeks. But with more and more of the infected showing up every day, from all directions now, he can't last forever.

And that's not going to change no matter how much help I try to offer. Best not to get too close. Not to get attached at all. I'm already doing too much by giving him time to catch up like this. I mount my horse and keep going forward as my mind wanders back a little ways.

* * *

I'd heard the wagons before I saw them. I wasn't on a trail, and the terrain, even though it's flat, would make for tough going for anything on wheels. The grass was shorter than on some prairies but it could catch in the spokes and build up, eventually causing snags for the wheels. Even if that didn't happen, the uneven clumps with tough stems would give travelers an even bumpier ride than the deep ruts of a heavily used trail.

The two wagons groaned and complained as they lurched along. I found a stand of brush a little out of their path before they got too close and made my horse stay very still behind the bushes. We hadn't known each other very long but he was a good horse. Mr. Lin knew everyone in that temporary-looking town, including the trader who sold it to me, and he'd made sure I got a fair deal on a healthy animal with a good temperament.

So we stood quietly off to the side, hopefully unnoticeable to the driver or anyone inside, to watch as this wagon train of two went by. As they came closer it was clear something wasn't right. No one sat on the driver's seat of either one, nor walked alongside them, but the horses—two to each cart—kept going. Looked like they'd bolted, if you could call their halting, labored progress over the grasses bolting. Their sides trembled with exhaustion and glistened with sweat; their eyes rolled in their heads.

Next I saw splatters of blood on the side of one of the wagons, starting on the wood and splashed up the cloth covering, which had already traded its white color for a gray-brown coating of dust even before it had been stained with blood. More dust had collected in the blood before it dried, I saw as it went past. I felt pity for the horses, but not enough to try and catch them and free them of their burdens.

Until I saw a hand trying to grip the back of the wagon from inside. It got jostled off and disappeared as the wagon flew over a bump, but I was sure I'd seen it.

I nudged my mount into motion and we went after them. It wasn't hard; the four horses were flagging. Despite their panic, one of them slowed as soon as I grabbed its reins, and when it stumbled to a stop, its partner followed suit right away.

I left them and they thankfully stayed put, chests heaving, heads hanging down, while I went after the other wagon and did the same. As I did, one of the first team of horses gave a whinny that sounded terrified despite being breathy and exhausted. I turned back and saw some movement at the front opening of the covered wagon.

One of the sick, a young man, scrabbling its way out. It ignored the horses—they never seemed to crave any kind of flesh but that of a human—and tumbled over the driver's seat onto the ground. It sensed me as it scrambled to its feet in the herky-jerky way they had. I met it halfway and dispatched it with my knife. It told me the young man's story as I braced my hand on the shoulder for leverage in order to bring the blade down into its skull. I never got the full sense of a person's life, just the worst things they'd ever done or the worst that had ever happened to them. This one had tormented the neighbor's simple oldest son, who he knew wouldn't be able to tell anyone, without mercy in secret for years, delighting in finding new, ever crueler tactics, until his own family had embarked on this journey.

I never got used to learning these things that other people were capable of. I pulled my hand away, shivering, and turned to the other figures that had begun to spill out of the two wagons. I got in a tight spot for a second when one of them knocked me to the ground and he and two others swarmed me. With my back against a wagon wheel I fended them off, trying to tamp down a rising panic as my arm seemed to throb warningly with the memory of teeth grinding down into my flesh.

I managed to draw my knees to my chest and kick one of them, so hard it fell on its back a few feet away. That knocked another one off balance enough that I could get out of their trap and out into the open. My arms were shaking by the time I dealt the last death blow to the trio. It wasn't good, this fear that got hold of me sometimes ever since I was bitten. I couldn't afford the momentary weakness that came with it.

The wagons were both silent now but I checked each one out—going slow and cautious because occasionally the infected seemed to lie in wait, or rather be in a kind of trancelike state until a living human tripped their senses and put them on the attack.

The first vehicle was empty of any humans, living or sick, so I moved to the other one.

Near the rear of this one, two bodies. I saw a shovel nearby them in the bed of the wagon and prodded them with it to see if they would come to life. When they didn't move I laid one of my hands on each of their backs and gave them a moment to tell me a story, but they were silent. My best guess as to why this happened is that only those that had done wrong, or been done wrong at the hands of another, had reason to come back when they were bit. Some folks just rested in peace when a sick one killed them. I reckoned there had to be people who got through the world skirting between doing evil and encountering evil, and no dead body had ever told me a story of a life like that, so I figured the silent ones were the lucky ones.

Just then one of them stirred a little, and I jumped backward, my heart knocking against the walls of my chest. The small movement repeated, both bodies this time, but it wasn't like the invisible string-puppet movement of a sick one coming to life. I got my knife in my hand and watched, ready to run or attack.

The movement happened again, and I heard a panting, like a living human, and then a little kid squeezed out from under the two dead bodies. A boy, from the looks of it, though it was hard to tell from the shaggy dirty locks of hair and baggy clothes. The eyes peering out from under his hair were wide and haunted. He scrambled the rest of the way out, then spotted me and scuttled backwards to the other side of the wagon.

"I ain't one of them," I told him, and he froze, staring. I started to say that he was safe now but reckoned that wasn't true, even if the immediate threat was gone. "You can come out if you want." I left him to make that decision for himself and went to rifle through the other wagon for supplies I could scavenge. I found some salted pork that looked unspoiled and two cans of peaches. I also came across a knife, smaller than mine and in an ancient-looking sheath but still with a sharp point and blade.

By the time I climbed out of that wagon and moved to the one with the two bodies in it, the kid had disappeared. I found some more food and a small bottle of liquor and added it all to my saddlebags.

"Mister, can you help me?" The small voice came from behind, and I turned to see him peeking out from under the wagon at me.

There was no one around but this kid, so I didn't much feel like putting on an act. "I ain't no mister, and I can't help," I said.

He wriggled partway out on his belly and looked at me with frank curiosity, in that amazing way a kid can just forget all their troubles, no matter how bad, if their brain latches on to a new puzzle or piece of information. "You a lady?"

I scoffed a little and shook my head. "I ain't a lady either."

He seemed to accept that pretty readily. That's another gift of young'uns, being able to take in a new idea without too much struggle. There are so many things they don't know about the world that surprising discoveries are a fairly regular occurrence. "Can you take me with you?" he asked. "My ma—my ma and pa—" His voice cracked and trailed off. His eyes widened and then brimmed with tears as the reality he'd managed to forget for a few moments came crashing back down on top of him.

I felt his pain like it was my own, like needles digging into every inch of my skin, but I clenched my jaw and shook my head.

I went to the horses and started to let them out of their harnesses and slap them away. They might survive. Maybe some Cheyenne or Arapaho would come across them, or some other settlers. My hands hesitated on the last animal, a little younger and smaller than the other three. I unhitched it but held onto its reins, and bent down to where the kid had crawled to the front of the underside of the wagon to watch me. "Bet you can't even ride a full-sized horse," I said dismissively.

"Bet you I can!" he protested, rising to my bait. He scrambled out of his shelter and grabbed the reins I held out to him.

"Good, then you can make it on your own," I told him. I ignored his arguments and lit out. I heard his horse's hooves behind me and increased my pace until they were more distant. Though I could still see him following whenever I glanced back, he made no attempt to close the gap between us, so I let my horse revert to an easy trot.

The kid waited until I was settled in with a fire and dinner before he caught up to me. I glared at him in the dusk and fireglow but he didn't leave, so I handed him some of the pork I'd fried up with the peaches on the side. "This came from your wagons so it's right you get a share," I told him. "But after this you need to go your own way."

He grabbed the plate and sat a short distance away. "Thanks, Mis—" He paused, chewing on a bite of meat. "What do I call you?"

I sighed. "Kit," I said, not bothering to make up a last name. It hit me all over again that I didn't have to make up names anymore; my last name was Goodwin. I'd read that name a thousand times on the wanted poster and wondered about the horse thieves it belonged to, but never thought they had any connection to me until Mr. Lin told me what the other side of the paper said.

"Kit," the boy repeated. "My name's Harvey." He picked up a peach slice and shoved it in his mouth, licking his fingers. "You goin' home?"

Good question. I didn't know and I didn't answer. I thought about asking him where he came from, what had happened, but I couldn't think of a question that wouldn't upset him and I didn't want to see that again.

"I'm goin' alone, is what I'm doin'," I said finally. "You get along as soon as you finish."

He slowed down the pace of his eating when he heard that, but he was too hungry to stop entirely and soon his plate was clean; he even licked the grease and peach juice off it.

"Now get out of here," I said as coldly as I could. Harvey stood, his thin shoulders hunched under his wild tangle of hair, and turned to his horse. "Hold up," I said, and he looked back at me.

I gave him my second canteen, which was half full of water. Then I produced the knife I'd found in the wagon.

"If you got no choice, stab them in the head as hard as you can," I said. "You gotta hit 'em just right, but if you do, it'll end 'em. It's the only thing that works." It was a lucky break that had taught me that trick, after I'd fought with the first one I ever encountered till I nearly ran out of strength. I shoved the knife toward Harvey and he took it, looking younger and more frightened than ever. "But your best bet is hide, just like you did back there. They don't seem to see or hear too good, and they can't smell you 'less you're pretty close to 'em and there's nothin' between you." I turned away. "Now *git*. I don't want to see you no more." I refused to look in his direction again until I heard him riding slowly away.

* * *

Now we have an unspoken deal. He stays out of my way, and I leave him food at mealtimes and clear the area in a wide circle around my campsite every night, dispatching any sick I see. I know I'm just helping drag his life out a little longer; at some point his luck's going to run out. But he's lasted this long, and it's not much more work to do what I do for him. It doesn't make him my responsibility, I tell myself. I could stop doing this tomorrow and my conscience would be clear.

Sometimes he leaves me a little figure of a man he's made by twisting sticks and dried grass together somehow. I find them resting by the fire. I left the first few behind, but I've started collecting them. I often think about burning them the next time I build a fire but I haven't yet. I just throw them in the rucksack where I keep my ruined note from my mother and a few other useless odds and ends I can't seem to rid myself of. A stray hairpin I found while rolling up my bed after Rosalie left that morning. The deputy badge Barrett pinned on me so the townspeople would listen to me when I was helping round them up for his big meeting. A packet of tea leaves Cooky pressed into my hand when I went to say goodbye. I don't intend to take the little straw men, but when I wake up and see one waiting for me, I find myself wondering if it's gonna be the last, and before I know it I've stowed it away.

There's no living humans out here. There's not even any signs they ever did live here, yet the sick are growing more numerous, coming from all sides. I watch for the kid and I feel more dread when he's out of sight. I curse myself for letting myself care this much. I'm determined not to let my feelings go any further.

* * *

One of the infected comes upon me one morning as I'm waking up. I never worry too much about sleeping because they don't seem to notice humans if they're not moving around or making noise, but maybe I was sleeping restless enough for this one to get a bead on me. My sleeping brain puts his snarling into a dream, and the dream scares me awake, and that's when I see him staggering toward me.

The fear sends a jolt of energy through me and I'm up and scrambling for my knife just as he gets within reach. He knocks me to the ground and we grapple with him on top of me. His terrible story is already flowing into my mind but I try not to get caught up in it; I've got to find my knife, which has fallen off to my right somewhere.

Then he goes limp, pinning me to the ground. A small gob of brains falls on my forehead as I see Harvey tugging his knife out of the sick one's head. Our eyes meet and then he's gone. Underneath my relief I feel an unwilling admiration—kid's tougher than he looks. I push the heavy body off me with distaste, the man's wicked deeds sliding through my consciousness like venom. I flick the fragment of his brain off my skin and scrub at my forehead with my sleeve as I get up.

This one smells odd. His clothes give off a smell like stagnant swamp water, damp rotting wood. I crouch and look closer at him. His hands and the front of his shirt have shreds of something slimy and mottled stuck to them. I reach out, curious, and just as I'm about to touch some of the substance I realize it looks like rotten flesh, but it doesn't come from *this* sick one—he's been freshly bitten and just come back. Too late to stop, my fingers come in contact with the stuff.

A rushing inside my head almost knocks me over again. This flesh is trying to tell me a story, and it's an old one. Lots of the misdeeds and injustices I learn about are from long ago, but this one has an extra feeling of distance, its exact meaning eluding my mind, drawing me down into the pain of a not-living thing that long ago lost its human faculties of thinking and understanding.

Despite that, despite not knowing what it is I'm feeling pain about, I feel it like it's my own. It's like every loss I've ever experienced wrapped up together and magnified. I pull my hand away and bend over, gripping my knees for support, as a wave of nausea sweeps over me. The feeling ebbs in strength now that I've lost contact with the remains, but it doesn't leave me completely. It's part of me now, and it saps my strength. I curl up on my blanket until it dissipates enough for me to be able to move again.

I pretend not to see the kid hovering a few yards away as I pack up to get going. I've got no appetite so I don't bother with breakfast, though I do leave a few crackers and a handful of dried fruit behind at the campsite.

* * *

That weakness stays with me for a while, but I manage to fend off the infected I come across. Harvey is following me more closely now, but I ignore him and he doesn't try to talk to me or catch my eye. It's somewhat comforting having him nearer, not only because it's easier to confirm he's still around but because he's saved my life once, and in my current state it feels more likely I might need help again.

What keeps me going even in my senseless grief over something I don't even understand is the pull toward where I'm going. It's seemed to double in power after that morning. Now my inner compass is exacting, sounding an alarm when I deviate even a little from the path it wants me to take. Once I'm back to full strength I travel longer periods of time each day, Harvey and both our horses showing exhaustion by the time I stop for the night. If not for them I'd keep going even later.

I don't feel tired or hungry anymore. Only Harvey's pale little face reminds me to cook and eat so I can leave something for him. He's in sight almost all the time now, although I still don't speak to or acknowledge him. He doesn't wait for me to leave in the afternoons before approaching and grabbing the lunch I've left for him, and I don't bother to feign sleep after dinner; he takes his share as I'm still setting up my bedroll.

* * *

My compass is stronger than ever. I can't tell if I'm imagining it, but the grasses in front of me seem to part, creating a visible path, their blades bending toward the east as if there's a strong wind at my back that's pushing them down. I want to ask Harvey if he sees it, but I don't break our mutual silence. I need all my attention anyway for what's ahead of me. Whatever it is, it is pulling me. Sometimes I swear the charm on my necklace lifts ever so slightly off my chest like a magnet is drawing it forward. When the feeling gets really strong, my hairs, even the tiny ones on my body, feel like they're all standing on end. It reminds me of a time when I was fourteen and narrowly missed being struck by lightning, except there are no clouds in the sky.

One day I don't stop for dinner. I don't stop for the night. My horse keeps going obediently, though its pace flags as it stumbles through the darkness. Our way is lit only by a full moon and thousands of stars.

The air around me grows thicker and closer. My ears are ringing and everything physical feels distant (including Harvey, who's right behind me but looks dim and unreal), while unseen things wrap around me and soak into my skin, into my senses.

Then a familiar smell—a real one, I think—invades my nostrils, and the physical world comes back to me. It's the swampy, rotten smell that radiated off that sick one's clothing. I dismount at the edge of a stand of trees and enter on foot, my eyes adjusting enough to see dimly despite the branches blocking out most of the moon and starlight.

There's a body of water—a small pond maybe. Stagnant, stinking, likely covered in scum and plant life, since there's no reflection on its surface of what moonlight does come through the overhanging leaves. It's mainly the smell and the cool damp feeling radiating from it that tell me it's water.

It gives off a rippling sound as if there's wind, or a tide—or something moving within it. Then it's still again. I tread carefully along the spongy earth at its edge. Ahead of me is a large spreading oak tree. The ringing in my ears, more like a buzzing now, gets louder. I touch the tree, as if I think it's going to tell me a story like the bodies of the infected do. It doesn't, of course, but it does feel like it's vibrating with energy, like there's a steam engine rumbling deep within it.

I withdraw my hand, unnerved, and keep walking. The big oak is the last tree in the cluster. Past it the moon becomes fully visible again, bathing the ground in cool white light. I spot something a few yards away, resembling pieces of wood sticking out of a pile of junk.

Moving closer, I realize it's a wagon, or the remnants of one. The axles have given way and the body of it rests on the ground, wheels lying on their sides or clinging to their broken axle and leaning at strange angles. The pieces of wood I saw are poles that once supported a canvas cover. Shreds of filthy, disintegrating cloth still cling to them here and there. It doesn't look like much, but it draws me as strongly as the water and the oak tree did. I stumble over bits of wood as I get closer. I feel the splintered, weathered boards under my hands as I rest them on the edge of the wagon bed and peer inside, my head and heart pounding.

Something rears up from the bottom of the wagon and I try to back away, but my heel catches on something, probably on the same boards I nearly tripped on before, and I'm on the ground, struggling to get up.

The thing leaps out of the wagon with a weird awkward grace like some kind of skinny long-limbed insect, tattered rags that might've once been a dress fluttering from its body. I'm frozen where I fell, unable to do anything but stare at the thing approaching me. It's not like any sick one I've ever seen. It's almost a skeleton, its flesh dry, desiccated. The eyes are not pale marbled orbs; they're gaping holes in the face. The withered skin has pulled away from the eye sockets, nose, and mouth, and the creature's teeth are visible as it snaps and snarls.

I put my hands up, but weakly. I'm not going to be able to defend myself in this state, I know that, but it almost feels like it doesn't matter. My compass is no longer pulling at me. I have no idea why it wanted me here, but I know I've arrived.

Seconds tick by so slow they feel like minutes as the skeletal creature starts to descend on me. Then time seems to stop altogether. For some reason I think back to the very first sick one I encountered, all the way back in California.

I was out mending a fence with one other farmhand, a cranky old coot who'd grown on me over the past year despite my best efforts to keep everyone at arm's length. He spotted it first; truth be told I often let Jud rest and did all the work myself when the farmer was out of sight, so my attention was focused on tying new wire between fence posts when I heard him swear. Spontaneous swearing wasn't out of the ordinary coming from him, so that didn't make me look up.

"What the hell is he doing?" That did catch my ear, and I raised my head. Stumbling toward us over the field was a man. At first he seemed drunk. Then we saw the blood soaking the front of his clothes, and the mangled wounds at his throat and belly.

"Get help!" Jud told me, and jumped the fence with surprising agility given how he was always complaining of being tired and achy. He hurried toward the wounded man and I started for the farm, but an unearthly sound stopped me in my tracks. I looked back, then raced toward the spot where Jud had fallen, the stranger bending over him as if whispering in his ear. Then the man looked up, and I saw his pale eyes—and the ragged dripping piece of Judd's ear clamped in his teeth.

I fought that stranger for what felt like an hour. How I didn't get bit I still don't understand, because I wasn't used to fighting and I didn't know how to subdue this creature that came at me again and again, not responding when I tried to talk to him, never seeming to flag or lose energy when I hit or pushed him. I didn't have a knife on me that day, but finally in desperation I snatched up the pliers I'd been using to cut lengths of wire for the fence, and I stabbed at him again and again. I knew it probably wouldn't do anything—he had two gaping wounds already that didn't seem to be slowing him down or even causing him any pain—but I kept going. He pinned me to the ground, and I brought the wire cutters down on his crown with a last desperate burst of energy. They cracked his skull and entered his brain.

The man sagged heavily on me, and it took every ounce of strength to push him off. As I did so—as my hand pressed against his cold skin—I had my first experience of the sick communicating to me. I learned the terrible things that had happened to him as a child; I felt the pain and injustice of it down through my bones.

I'd relive many other people's past tragedies and misdeeds in the months to come, and it never got any easier than that first time, though at least I grew to know what to expect.

Jud was already dead by the time I got to his side. I knelt beside him in shock as he told me his own tragic past through my hand on his neck, knowing I had to get help but unable to move.

And then he wasn't dead anymore.

It didn't take me long to understand on some level what had happened, and that I had to use the same method to stop Jud before he could rip my guts out like the stranger had done to him.

As hard as it was, I didn't feel guilty afterward. But I also knew, as I took a step back, what it looked like had happened. Two men dead, torn to pieces, skulls crushed in. A third man still alive, with bloody pliers and a blood-soaked shirt.

I snuck back to my quarters, a lean-to off the main house. (I'd convinced the farmer to let me build it a few weeks after I arrived, after being put in the bunkhouse first and feigning loud snoring and night terrors until the other men insisted I leave.) I knew which field the farmer had everyone else working that day. His wife would be busy inside cooking lunch.

I changed clothes, tied up my bloody ones in a bundle to dispose of later, and took my few belongings — a few other scraps of clothing, my saved-up wages, the wanted notice with its blood-written note and the necklace, not much else. I rode hard that day, knowing I'd be a wanted man by the evening at the latest, or whenever the bodies were discovered.

And once I started riding, I started feeling that tug that I'd come to think of as my compass.

That night, I felt compelled to note the two men's passing somehow, and I made the first two of many tattoos on my arm.

The memory of that bloody beginning of my journey flashes through my mind in a brief window of frozen time before the sick one from the ruined wagon descends on me. Its bony, brittle chest collides with my outstretched hands. Everything disappears.

Or rather, it doesn't disappear so much as transform. I sit up and look around. I'm in the same place but it's sunset, not midnight anymore. The covered wagon is restored — battered and dirty from travel but looking like new compared with its state a moment ago. The oak tree seems smaller but its leaves are fuller, like it's later in the season than when I arrived.

The creature is gone, but I'm not alone. There are several men standing under the oak tree, two of them more boys than grown men, three of them (including the young ones) with ropes around their necks. There's a woman too.

A heavily pregnant woman, face contorted, snot and tears running down her face, her hair and eyes wild. I can't hear anything over the ringing-buzzing sound in my ears, but I somehow know what she and the others are saying when their mouths move. Everyone seems to be moving slower than what would be possible in real life, but the warmth on my skin feels real as I sit in the scrubby patch of grass between the wagon and the oak tree, unable to move.

Unable to help as the man and boys are hanged, as the woman is shot, as the murderers take their horses and leave after dumping the men in the water. Unable to provide any comfort as the woman bleeds out slowly while giving birth alone, as she dips a twig in blood and scrawls weakly on the back of the paper that served as her family's death warrant. As she nurses her newborn and wraps it carefully in her shawl, then cradles it as her life drains away.

I watch the baby become restless, suckling fruitlessly, struggling against the swaddling, starting to cry. I watch a man come and take the baby from the woman's lifeless arms and walk away with it. I can't follow; I can only watch him and his companion slowly disappear from view.

I look back at the dead woman, and something shifts. She opens her eyes, but she doesn't look infected. She smiles at me, not a carefree smile but not entirely unhappy either. She rises and comes over to where I'm frozen in place.

I notice her dress is no longer bloody as she kneels in front of me. She reaches for me and pulls my head toward her, coaxing me to rest on her still-full breasts and belly. She strokes me and it's like the sun reaching down and caressing me with its rays. I close my eyes as the warmth spreads through me.

I open them again and look past her to see the man and two youths rise from the pond. They're dripping wet but seemingly unharmed, and by the time they reach me and the woman, their clothes and hair are dry. I feel the man come up behind me, sit down, and put his arms around my waist, leaning his head against mine as it leans on the woman's chest. The two boys kneel next to me; one takes my hand between his, the other brushes my hair out of my eyes, which feel hot with unshed tears. I can't speak, but their smiles show that they know their love is reaching me.

My grief for them is joined by something else. I can feel them drawing it out into the open from long-closed dusty corners of my mind. I struggle against it but their persistent caresses disarm me, and soon I succumb to pain I'd successfully blocked out for well over a year.

* * *

My adoptive mother saw it coming and, in her way, tried to warn me. I knew I wasn't like my brother, and it wasn't just because he was stout and blond and ruddy-faced while I was skinny and short with dark hair and sallow skin that tanned easily. What I didn't fully understand, which she didn't know how to tell me but sensed instinctively, was the danger my difference posed for me.

She couldn't talk about what was happening to me, to tell me the changes I was going through were more like her own when she was a girl than what my brother was going through as he became a man. She tried not to treat me differently, but she was always telling me to keep my shirt and undershirt on, even when my brother and father stripped to the waist doing farm work on hot days.

She did tell me, when I came to her worried because my stomach was in pain and there was blood in my drawers, that I wasn't sick but that I needed to make sure no one else saw the blood. From then on we were co-conspirators in a plot I only vaguely understood; she'd help me wash out and hide the rags I used to soak it up once a month.

The worry in her eyes made me take the other things she'd been telling me more seriously, and I made sure to keep my body covered and unseen by anyone, even my brother. I still didn't realize how dangerous it was, my change, but I got the hint that it was something I needed to keep between me and my mother.

Which worked until I was at a swimming hole with some of the boys from the neighboring farms and I insisted on keeping my undershirt on. They teased me about it but didn't much care. Until I came out of the water, the thin fabric plastered to my chest. Then everything changed. I saw in their eyes what they thought I was, what they thought they were going to take from me.

When they pinned me down and got my drawers off, the looks changed from hunger to disgust and rage. I didn't fully understand bodies, but I knew mine wasn't quite male or female. They were as angry at themselves for having wanted me as they were at me for being what I was, probably, but I was the only one they punished for it all.

It wasn't the beating I endured from them that day, or the fast-spreading rumors in our community, or the ongoing torment of them and other boys in the area, that hurt the most.

It was the day my father came home from a trip to town, glaring at me like I was a stranger who'd broken into his house. When he took my mother into their bedroom to talk privately but every word came to my ears through the thin wall. What he called me, how he talked about me. It was when I learned he'd never really considered me his child.

Later that night my mother, with red-rimmed eyes, took me out to the barn and showed me the paper and the necklace. Told me what little she knew about my start in life. Made me understand, without telling me, that I could not stay, either in my family or in the community.

She'd brought a length of cloth, and she made me practice wrapping it around my chest until I could create the necessary illusion under my shirts.

As I perfected the binding, I began to create a shell around myself. I understood that I was going to be all I had, maybe for the rest of my life. Whoever the woman was who'd been found dead with a little baby in her arms, whoever had scrawled an unintelligible note on the back of a wanted handbill and wrapped it in my swaddling, was gone. The people who'd rescued me and kept me alive were gone. My adopted family, my mother who had probably always sensed I was different but had tried to love me anyway, they were now gone too, and it was best not to let anyone else get through my shell.

My father took my brother out to work the fields the next morning without a single word to me, and I never saw them again. My mother clung to me and cried before I got on my horse, but I knew things had changed between us too. Underneath her sadness, I could see the relief in her eyes that the burden of trying to protect me was being lifted from her shoulders. I assumed that weight myself, and I arranged my features so she wouldn't see and be haunted by the pain I was feeling.

I never saw her again either. I thought about writing and sending money, once I got the job at the farm, but then I'd imagine the anger it might cause if my father saw it, and I never did. She'd taken on more than she bargained for when she agreed to take that baby boy from the trader's wife, but she'd tried to do right by me. The best way I could repay her was to let her be.

I pour all of this into the figures surrounding me, holding me, and their sadness and anger for my past joins and compounds what I'm feeling for theirs. They make me understand, in some way beyond words or rational thought, that my pain had reached them in their graves, fused with theirs, and grown inside them so that they spread it to others. Those who had felt or caused great enough pain also passed it along, and so that response to my pain had been traveling slowly toward me, fueled by the evil and suffering of others, and pulling me back toward them, to where I'd been born and they'd died all on the same day.

It's horrifying, the thought that in my attempt to close off and not ever affect any other human again, I'd somehow caused a cascade of death and suffering throughout the land. But it's also inexpressibly comforting to be in the arms of people who would've loved me if they'd been given a chance—who did grow to love me even in death, somehow, and felt my suffering from hundreds of miles away.

I don't know how long I stay in this state— time has ceased to have any meaning, and I have no sense of urgency or survival any more. But I gradually become aware of a voice calling my name.

At first I think it's one of my family, finally speaking out loud after saying so much through silent communion. But then I recognize the voice, and the buzzing in my ears begins to fade so I can hear it much more clearly.

"Kit, get up! Kit! They're coming for us!"

I can move again, and I lift my head, and the late summer sunset collapses into pitch blackness. Whether or not it was real or in my imagination, my eyesight still takes time to adjust. Before I can see anything, my nose once again detects that stagnant pond water smell, very close to me. My skin comes back to the present moment and instead of dry, soft clothes and warm skin against me I feel skeletal things pressed into me, wet and slimy on one hand, dry and withered on the other. My eyes adjust and I know that I'm surrounded by four creatures, the one who leapt out of the wagon and three that must've emerged from the water.

They sit with me still, holding me with their bony, ruined arms and bodies, and though I feel no horror upon seeing what they really are, I can only imagine what it looks like for Harvey. He's dancing from foot to foot, afraid to come too close, looking behind him and then back at me. "Kit, what's happenin'? We gotta get out of here!"

I can't ignore his plea or the terror on his face. I gently extricate myself from the four creatures that somehow exude love for me despite their terrible eyeless sockets and exposed teeth. They don't resist, and when I leave their arms, they come closer together, holding one another silently and still.

But the rest of the area isn't silent or still. As I shake myself from my stupor, all around us I hear snarling, the crackling of twigs, and the rustling of grass and leaves. We're surrounded and being borne down upon from all sides.

Water splashing joins the other sounds and I see the surface of the pond is rippling and being disturbed. Creatures emerge from it, even more ruined than my family, little more than skeletons, some with no scalp at all, others with patches of hair still matting their head.

Of course my family wasn't the first one. I could just imagine their murderers lying in wait each time, knowing the people they'd just pretended to help would be passing by this very spot with its small but deep pond that made for a convenient mass grave and the oak with the thick sturdy bough that ran parallel to the ground just above head level, perfect for stringing nooses over.

"Kit there's too many! What are we gonna do, Kit?" Harvey wheels around and just barely evades a sick one; its clumsy lunge is successful only in sending it tumbling to the ground. The boy drives his knife deep into its skull with both hands and tugs it out again with strength born of panic.

I turn in a slow circle, watching as the sick from the pond and from all around us close in. Suddenly I'm filled with rage at Harvey. If he weren't here, I know exactly what I'd do. I'd let the sick get me and, since I couldn't seem to be killed or turned from one bite, I'd hope that they eventually inflicted enough damage to my body that I could just die, right here next to my family. Which is probably what should've happened in the first place, years ago, if my mother Maisie hadn't fought so hard to bring me into the world and keep me alive.

But Harvey *is* here, and I know what I have to do instead. Or at least I know I have to try, and hope it works. If it doesn't, he'll have to die with me, and it'll serve him right for trying to attach himself to me, a mistake of creation who's never belonged in this world or with other living people.

I return to my family. They look up at me with their empty eyes. They are different from any other sick; at least they're different around me. I meet their gaze. "I'm sorry," I whisper. I can't speak properly through the lump in my throat. My eyesight grows dim with tears and I scrub my eyes with my sleeve repeatedly to clear my vision, though it blurs over each time almost as soon as I do. I take my knife out of its sheath. My hands are trembling and I think I can't do it. Then I hear Harvey cry out and I act before I even know it.

I take out my brothers first, then my father. My mother's ruined skeletal face somehow looks twisted in agony, but she doesn't move, doesn't struggle or attack me or try to run away. She reaches up and touches the silver charm dangling from my neck, and as her skin like dead lichen brushes against my collarbone, I somehow know from her that the symbol on it means eternal love. I lift my knife one last time and bury it deep within her skull.

She collapses on top of my brothers and father. I don't have to work to dislodge my knife; her head crumbles away from it and I lift it easily. Before my eyes, all four of them disintegrate, melting into the ground until there's nothing but a small heap of ragged clothing remnants, indistinguishable as separate garments.

I tear my eyes away from that sight and see that all around us, the sick that were approaching have collapsed. I feel relief but not euphoria that the sickness is seemingly gone. I'm mainly thinking about how it's safe to turn my blade on myself now, and I wonder what's the fastest, most surefire way of killing yourself with a knife.

I turn in another slow circle and end on Harvey. At times he's seemed almost like an adult, tough and determined. That's all gone now. What's left is a shattered little boy with dark circles under his teary eyes, thin shoulders sagging with exhaustion and shock as he too surveys the bodies littering the area around us.

Later, when I leave, I'll realize the extent of it. Like shards of metal to a magnet, the infected were approaching from all sides in the hundreds, and their bodies cover the ground like trees felled by a massive wind. Much will be written about this in newspapers as one reporter telegraphs it to others, but it'll soon be dismissed as a hoax or mass hysteria.

But I'm not thinking of any of that yet. I sheathe my knife and kneel beside Harvey. "Hey," I say. His eyes are glassy; he doesn't respond. I scoop him up and carry him to my horse. His is there too, right next to mine. I put a lead on his mount, set the kid in front of me on my horse, and start riding. Harvey's body sags against me, and I hope it helps him feel safe at last. I don't know where I'm going, but as the sun rises behind us I can tell we're heading west.

ACKNOWLEDGMENTS

This is a work of fiction—paranormal at that—so I felt free to toy with exact historical timelines, geography, and other details to suit my story. But in my research I encountered historical figures whose DNA exists in a couple of my characters: Lucy / Joseph Lobdell, whose fluid gender and sexuality led to hardships and persecution in the 1800s; and Lim Lip Hong, a self-made man who immigrated to the U.S. at age 12 and became one of the first Chinese people hired for the building of the Central Pacific Railroad. Lobdell's endurance and nonconformity and Lim's strength and resourcefulness inspired me immensely as I wrote the characters of Kit and Lin.